The Wild Cat

Taanya Sarma

First published in USA in 2017

ISBN: 978-93-87328-13-6

Invincible Publishers
G-120, Sushant Lok III, Sector 57, Gurgaon-122002

Registered Address: Opposite Kasturba Ashram, Radaur, Haryana - 135133

CONTENTS

CHAPTER ONE

The Wild Cat

The sun traced its way halfway across the floor as I came to the realization that it was late in the morning. I stared at the ceiling and pondered how I could make time tick by a little faster. While others eagerly anticipated the weekend, to me, Saturday and Sunday were the two longest and loneliest days of the week. Wallowing in my own boredom, I felt reluctant to cook, let alone do my dishes or forget about even going out.

Bah - another long weekend!

Instinctively, my eyes cut down and gazed upon the spectacle known as my body. Loneliness sucks - especially at this time of the year. Don't get me wrong or go feeling sorry for me; I get a decent sum of dinner invites, but managing life is a tedious task.

Our mind is an easy thing to mold in accordance with what is happening at the present moment; whereas, the heart tends to cling to the past. I decided to motivate and ascend from my horizontal position into a vertical one.

I nudged the mouse pad with the tip of my finger and awakened my laptop from its slumber. I opened my browser and scanned the familiar news feed on CNN. Nothing but the same boring, uneventful nonsense. No excitement whatsoever. I couldn't help but think how

CNN should stand for 'Constant Negative News', but at this moment they were broadcasting the CNN hero awards. I wanted something earthly, something truly newsworthy. The Macy's Thanksgiving Day Parade in NYC - not my style either. I gave up after working the channel button on the clicker for a few minutes. I placed the remote on the table and finally got up as the TV roulette ended up landing on a QVC bit about some sort of food slicer.

My mind and body united long enough to bring awareness to the fact that I was wandering around the room aimlessly in my PINK Victoria's Secret pajamas for no apparent reason. I was in search of something, but I wasn't exactly sure what that something was. Was it something - or was it someone?

I stood in a ray of sunlight as I peered outside my window, with no shame in the fact that I was half naked. This cold weather makes me lazy and reluctant to do anything at all. Fallen leaves were levitating in the pool.

As I looked away from the window, I scanned my room one last time. My eyes focused on a box hiding behind some books on the white IKEA shelf. I sauntered across the room and pulled the box from the shelf and then planted myself down like a cement block with this newfound treasure in my lap. I picked it up and with a quick exhale through pursed lips, blew the dust from the box top. This was no ordinary box, rather a memory box containing hundreds of cards and other things from my school days. I carefully removed the lid and then released each memory from its tomb as I gave them life by reading each one out loud. I vividly contemplated that time of my life, but things are different now. I was, however, impressed by the self-realization that I, even as a young, innocent girl, managed to still have dozens of pen pals. I smiled as I uncovered a picture of me and a friend posing cheek to cheek with a cheesy smile on our faces. I flipped the photo over and written on the back was a note in, I could only assume, my friend's handwriting. The loopy, cursive text read "BFF's - best friends forever!"

Just then, my momentary nostalgia was interrupted by the phone ringing on other side of the room. I made haste, but paused for a split second to glance at the caller ID and catch my breath before answering. My phone didn't recognize the number, so my curiosity was aroused.

"Hello" I answered timidly, fully expecting to hear an automated invitation to update my free Google listing or buy a timeshare or something equally undesirable at the moment. Instead, I was pleasantly surprised.

"Is this Tanya?" the voice on the other end of the phone inquired.

I gathered courage to utter a timid greeting, "Yes, this is Tanya."

"Hey Tanya! It's been so long. This is Dorothy. You didn't forget me, did you, girl?"

Before I could even respond, Dorothy continued with a rapid-fire line of questioning. I guess when you haven't spoken in a while; thoughts and emotions get pent up.

"Where have you been? So, there is this house party tonight. Let's catch up there. I am sure A.J. has already invited you." I noticed a sudden change in her voice as her excitement faded away. "Oh-M-Geee, I'm so sorry, you must still be in grief. I overheard my dad talking about the accident." Dorothy proceeded to carry on and on about the death of my parents.

My mom died at a very young age, and I don't remember her at all. The only memories I have of her were relayed to me through stories and comments from my father. He described her as an artistic and beautiful, loving person. I'm glad my father shared these details about my mother with me before he recently passed away in a car crash. This untimely tragedy occurred while I was attending my last semester at Duke University, working towards my MBA.

Frustrated and overwhelmed by emotion, and no longer able to tolerate her ranting, I hung up on Dorothy and then quickly stuffed everything back in the memory box. I then scanned the room and found a place to hide it where it could never be found.

I found myself frantically crying while putting on a dress. I moved swiftly towards the front door and rushed towards my car. I drove up and down and all across the enormous city. Exhausted and disenchanted from driving any further, I decided to spend the rest of my night at our gallery down the road near MaxWell Shopping Center. I had to park my car on 43rd street and take a short but chilly walk in the bitterly cold air. It was worth everything, to have that feeling of being home.

This gallery was my dad's first among seven others across the state. He had so much love for art and crafts, but he was not an artist himself; however, he recognized one when he met one. That is exactly how he fell in love with my mom.

I managed to open the lock with my numb fingertips. It's weird, but I have this thing where my nails turn blue so easily.

As the door flung open, I was relieved to feel the warmth from inside. Apparently, I must have had left the heat running yesterday. I made my way into the gallery and toward the very back where there was a 120-volt breaker box. I quickly flipped the breakers labeled 1-16 to the on position and illuminated the gallery to the corner to keep people from thinking that the gallery was open today. Dealing with customers or the general public wasn't on my agenda today, so they would all have to wait until my staff joined back on Monday afternoon.

The fluorescent lights flickered for a moment and then their glow lit up, showing the path to my dad's office. My fingers were numb and still blue, and I needed to get warm. As I opened the door to the office, I heard someone banging on the front door. I closed my eyes tightly and established a grip on the door knob. Although I had no intention of answering the front door at the time, I quickly guilted myself into thinking that I should. After all, that is what my dad would have wanted me to do.

With my confidence and composure gathered to the best of my ability, I walked confidently and with all my force to the front door. As I approached the glass storefront, the person at the front door became clearly visible. She was wearing a red dress with a fur coat. Damn, it was Dorothy! I opened the door quickly to prevent her from further freezing out in the winter weather. I surprised myself at how quickly I could gulp down my emotions and put on a poker face. I think this ability comes from doing business on a daily basis. Now it has become part of my personality. I put a smile on and... here you go. The goal for me is to keep the person across from me from ever knowing what's troubling me.

I hugged her and walked her through the door. She pushed me away and demanded "Get ready, you are coming with me."

I pulled myself away. "No, Dorothy, I am not."

"Yes, you are. No excuses - I have an extra dress and makeup in my car. You are coming with me."

There was no point in reasoning with her. She's got her own perspective, plus the money and all the time in her life she desires to waste on parties. I never understood why she dragged me into her events and things. I tried my best to avoid her, but she always managed to reemerge in my life like a boomerang or a crazy ex.

She shoved me into a limousine that was parked out front and once we were on our way, she stripped me and put me into a short, black dress right there in the back of the limo. Black is not my color, but I managed to just go with the flow. There was nothing to lose! I'm not easy going and I'm way too stubborn, but still, I love this crazy girl - no matter how crazy she is. I felt empathy for her in light of the fact that she just went through a recent separation. I hate to see relationships fail, but I was glad she had the courage and resources to get out of her abusive marriage. Her worst half beat her black and blue for the final time.

Dorothy always tends to worry about others more than herself (unless there are men around that she is trying to attract). She looked at me like a mother looks at her child while getting them ready for school. She proceeded to grill me about things I do and don't do while she put the finishing touches on my makeup and nails.

"Why do you pretend to be a homeless person? You've got money, great taste in clothing and a luxurious style, but you dress so simple. Get it together, girlfriend!"

She was right, but I wasn't in the mood to field those questions, so I changed the subject.

"If I may ask, how far is this house party? Why are we driving out of town?" I always doubted her and needed reassurance that her plans were copacetic.

She quickly came clean with her intentions. "Ah! I am actually going to meet a guy. I have been dating him over the phone. I am in love with his voice and he sounds so handsome. I have physical needs and I can't wait forever for something to happen. So I'm about to make something happen!"

I was a little shocked by what she revealed - especially considering she had only been separated a few months and her divorce was not even finalized.

"Dorothy, have you been dating online?" I tried to reconcile how she was ready to be going on a date with physical needs on her mind.

"Yes. I am dating online. I found this new app that matches you with a person of similar interests and lets you talk to them in a group or one on one."

"So, how long have you been talking to this guy?" Surely, I figured, it couldn't have been too long.

Dorothy admitted, "It's been two weeks."

"Oh my God - two weeks! I know you are crazy, but this is insane. Did you do a background check on this guy?" I sensed that she was about to go into defense mode, so I changed my tone. "Look, I'm just asking because I worry about you."

Yet her response still conveyed indifference. "Who cares!" she said with a slight eye roll.

"I care - and I'm not coming and I'm not letting you go either." I folded my arms and was determined to hold firm on this, no matter what.

She flashed a nonchalant smile, "Tanya, there's nothing to worry about - he doesn't even know what I look like."

"Do you know what he looks like?" I was sure she didn't, but I had to ask.

"No, but I asked him to wear red Jockey underwear!" She said as she bit the corner of her lip in a most erotic fashion.

"What the hell, Dorothy - are you going to check every guy's under pants in the room?" I turned red with embarrassment as soon as I asked the question.

She laughed with a wink, "I don't mind. You can close your eyes or you can help!"

We soon stopped at this gigantic villa which looked like an adventure island gone rogue. I was awestruck at the size of the house and the crazy decor. Dorothy casually lit a cigarette and took a puff to relax herself as we prepared to make our grand entrance. That's just so typical of her. She knows I don't drink or smoke on a regular basis. I think the last time I touched alcohol was at my graduation party. "Did you drag me here so that I can take you home?"

"Come here!" she demanded as she grabbed me by my arm, spun me around and proceeded to kiss me in front of the doorman and a few partygoers.

Great, here she goes again. She can't help herself but grab and kiss me. She has a habit of grabbing people at awkward places and at the most unexpected times. It seemed tonight would not be an exception. I appreciated that she, in her own special way, respected my insecurities - I just wish that God would put some sense in her!

We walked into the party and past a bunch of malnourished, half-clad spoiled brats who were filling their lungs and the air with habit forming drugs and whatnot. It was obvious that the host had put a lot of planning and detail into the party. The ambiance was topped off appropriately with trance music playing at a lounge-level volume. If the host's goal was to get girls naked, it worked, as some of the brats we had just passed decided to drop their clothes and dance about in the buff. This reaffirmed just one of the many reasons why I don't indulge myself in any habit-forming substances. I don't get high on sugar, caffeine, cigarettes, alcohol, or even religion, sex or love; however, I have discovered that the latter two are equally habit forming.

The house music reverberated in my ears and the bass pounded in my chest. It was a nice party, but I quickly remembered why I opted not to go to parties most of the time. In fact, if I wasn't always sober and playing the designated driver's role (which my friends always impose on me and assume that I will gladly take), I probably wouldn't ever get invited to go anywhere.

Dorothy quickly found several reasons to abandon me. I loved her, but it seemed that all she ever cared about was getting attention from the guys. Based on history, I speculated that she probably won't even find the guy in the red Jockeys before she finds someone else to get affection from.

I took a walk around the pool and then through the beautifully landscaped back yard. I just wanted some alone time away from the party crowd, so I found a ledge to sit on next to some hedges, and I leaned back and looked skyward. The view was phenomenal. The night sky was clear and extra dark which made the millions of stars even more evident against the pitch-black backdrop. Minutes faded into hours as I lost myself in deep, meditative thought in my solitude. My senses finally re-entered reality and I decided that I should go and check in with Dorothy as she was probably looking for me and worried.

I realized that I must have really lost track of time and stayed in the yard much longer than I thought because the party had already started winding down. I found Dorothy draped all over some guy. He could have been the red Jockey guy or someone else - I didn't care and it appeared that she was happy regardless. What was disappointing to me was that she didn't even realize that I had been absent from the party pretty much the entire night. Someone could have slipped me a roofie, dragged me into the bushes to rape me and Dorothy wouldn't have noticed.

Dorothy informed me that she intended to go home with this guy after the party, so she walked me to the limo and sent me home solo. As the limo drove me back into the city, I realized for the very first time that the nightlife really looked amazing. Out of this world, in fact! Just like in the movies King Kong or Dark Knight. Tall buildings with twinkling lights illuminated the black backdrop of the night sky. I could see the reflections on my window passing by.

The limo driver looked back at me through his rear-view mirror and sensing that I might like some fresh air, he rolled down the window. I felt the winter cold slap me in the face. I pondered where the people we passed were going and what they were thinking. Maybe they were heading back to their loved ones after work. It's such a big world with so many wide roads interconnecting us, but all of a sudden, I felt a renewed love for the city that I had called home for so long.

It didn't take long for us to reach my house. The limo driver was a gentleman and came around to open my door.

I decided to open an account on iVoice with the intent of ushering Dorothy out of it. I figured that keeping an eye on her may help. She had been in so much trouble lately and I wanted to keep tabs on her so that I could be there for her if she needed me. Truth be told, maybe there were other things that I was seeking out of this app, but at the present moment, I had no clue. Certainly, I was not looking for earthly pleasures - I mean, how can you be in love or be intimate with a voice, while not knowing anything about that person. What if that person smells like weed or picks his nose or does not wash his hands after peeing? That, plus a thousand other factors, made the notion of falling in love online seem improbable and gross! Geez, how do people do it?

I searched for iVoice on the app store and downloaded it onto my phone. It was a very simple, one click process. I was just required to enter a nickname (which I pondered over for a bit), a password and email address - that was it and then I was all done - at least for the moment. The fun really began thereafter. I then had to fill out my entire preference sheet plus give access to my internet search history. Sharing my browsing history gave me a little anxiety, but I relented and granted the access anyway. I was a good girl and had nothing to be ashamed of.

The standard app profile was neutral in color with shades of dusty brown. I updated mine with a tattoo as the profile picture. I thought maybe I should put my puppy Maggy as my display picture (DP). Although she is a puppy, she already weighs 70 lbs. She is an adorable mix of Lab and German Shepherd and she is the cutest little thing on earth! I love her till death do us apart.

I read the terms of use agreement for this software. Yes, I'm a nerd in that aspect, but this technology was foreign to me and I wanted to make sure I knew what I was getting into. According to the user agreement, this software had been programmed and designed to turn off your device's web cam when the app is in use. After reading the terms of use in its entirety, I reluctantly clicked the 'I agree' button to activate my account and officially make my profile live.

I held my breath as I nervously logged in to my live account for the first time. The event was anti-climactic as I was directed to record my voice for about 30 seconds into the voice recognition system before I could go any further. Once this was done, the app created an account based on my voice. Apparently, this prohibits a person from having duplicate accounts. My voice recording was then further enhanced by the system to make it untraceable to a person - living or dead. The app was very complicated, but I at least felt like it was complicated for my own protection.

Now that I was in and official, I began to explore the app and its many features. There were so many ways to upload profile images or send gifts. The creator of the app found a unique way to profitize the software by charging a dollar to enhance your profile or send a gift to someone. I could enhance my profile into unlimited options, but of course, at a price. The more enhanced your profile is, the better the odds of you attracting someone to chat with you. As I browsed further into the app, it revealed channels where a group of people are given a collective space to talk.

Oh man, this was just too complicated for me and overwhelming at first. I decided to just enter a channel and observe. I was sure people would help me understand how it worked. At first, I had to enter a channel that the software picked for me based on my preferences. I entered quietly and was content to speak when it was my turn. I took a sip of water and nervously gulped it down, and then leaned closer to the mic on my phone as I prepared to introduce myself.

"Hi, I'm Iron Angel. I'm new to this app and this is my first group chat."

I wasn't prepared for the immediate and overwhelming response to my voice. In an instant, the channel went crazy and admirers started to shower me with gifts and invitations for private channel sessions. Wow, I was going to have to catch on to this program fast to keep up!

Each gift came with a string attached - a question for me to answer. I guessed this was how interaction took place. So I read along and tried to keep up with the barrage of questions that followed. I tried to answer each question promptly, respectfully and honestly.

I understand that people want to create an everlasting impression, but oftentimes while doing so, they become pretentious. Actually, I really don't believe in question and answer interview style sessions as an effective way to get to truly know a person. It was clear to me that this style of communication gives the person an opportunity to tailor their answers and put a spin on their response in a fashion that conveys what the person asking the question really wants to hear, more so than the honest truth. Hence, I felt it was easier to pretend than to be genuine. But that didn’t stop me from playing along.

Oh my God, I lost track of time and talked for almost three hours, but they still were not done with me. I let go of the group conversation and the next person in line promptly said, “She has such a sweet voice, but I couldn't understand a word of what she said because I was so lost in the beauty and honesty of her tone.”

Some users sent me virtual flowers with a note tag stating that the person after me was a 40-something, divorced man.

Being an ‘ambivert’ personality type and having been blown away by the outpouring of communication, gifts and offers for private chats that I had received, I decided that I should probably take precautions to protect myself, so I spent another hour going through the app tutorials and talking to customer service to understand how to block people. I couldn't understand why I was not allowed to block people permanently.

I got a slight lump in my throat as my message alert dinged and I realized that a user had just reached out to me for a private conversation and finally, I was ready to chat.

"Hi Iron Angel, I'm Adam. You have an interesting nickname - is it from a book or a movie?"

He picked the perfect ice-breaker and his question was of great interest to me, which made it easy for me to swallow the lump in my throat and respond with confidence.

"Hi Adam, thanks for asking. I actually borrowed my nickname from the movie Iron Jawed Angels. It's a great movie, you really must watch it."

His response was swift and appropriate. "Sure thing. Let me find the trailer real quick and watch it. I'll be right back with you."

The line went silent. I was impressed that he took the initiative to explore this movie so quickly - it showed me that he really cared about what interested me. This was a big feather in his cap so far.

A couple of minutes of silence transpired - just enough time for him to watch a two-minute movie trailer, then his voice came back across the line. "I watched the movie trailer. It looks more like a documentary movie."

I quickly replied, "It is. If you watch it, you'll get a good idea about me and my interests."

"Well, I don't need to watch a documentary movie to know some things about you. I noticed you have a puppy as your profile pic - you must like dogs. And you must be a women's rights activist since you chose a suffragist movie as your nickname. I'm very interested and intrigued!"

I blushed and smiled at the same time. I was flattered that this new online friend was taking interest in me and was noticing things about me that were important to me. I wanted to keep the conversation going.

"Yes, I do love my puppy - and I'm a very strong and independent woman. You are right; the movie is a documentary which is based on true stories that took place back before women could vote."

I didn't know if he was serious and would follow through, but he told me that he would add the movie to his watch list. I would be highly impressed if he actually watched the entire movie.

There was a long, awkward silence after this, so I prepared to continue the conversation further. I really wanted to get to know this guy more because it's rare to meet someone online that isn't a jerk or inappropriate - and the fact that he genuinely took interest in me was an added bonus.

"So Adam, tell me more about yourself."

"Well, what would you like to know? Feel free to ask me anything you want."

I didn't expect to get an open invitation to ask him anything I wanted. I decided to play it safe and ask a basic and innocent question that most users lead off with or ultimately ask. "How long have you been using this app?"

"Over a decade."

"That's a very long time."

"It was different at first. I cybered a lot back then. All day long sometimes - maybe 4 to 5 times a day on average."

I was perplexed. I had never heard that term before, so I asked, "What is Cybered?"

"Cyber Sex."

I wasn't expecting that response from this guy - at least this soon. I prefer to keep any sort of sex talk private, at least until we've actually been on a date. "Eww. Who does that? That's crazy!"

"It's actually not uncommon at all. There are so many social platforms with live feeds that allow cybersex activity." He said in defense of his habit.

I pondered the notion of spending all day cyber sexing. "How old are you, Adam?"

"Take a guess."

I paused and thought for a moment. "30 to 35?"

"You are close, I am 38."

"Are you married? Do you have any kids?"

"I am married, but I don't have any kids."

"How does your wife feel about this? Have you ever gotten caught? Are you addicted to cybersex?"

I really expected him to answer with some lame excuse or try to dodge the question, but he immediately came clean - and I appreciated his honesty.

"I want to be honest with you, but I don't want to scare you away. Yes, I am addicted. My therapist said I have to keep it under control. I show signs of perversion and voyeuring. Do you still want to keep the conversation going?"

His confession did change my opinion of him, but I really was impressed by his honesty. Rather than retreat from a sexual conversation as I usually do, I decided to play this one differently, so I responded accordingly. "Look, I am not here to judge anyone. This is all virtual and not part of my real life." I paused for a moment and wondered if this online life would ever merge with my actual life. I also couldn't help but wonder why a married man would be on this site. The human mind and its complexity as well as the diversity in which people think, fascinates me. I snapped out of my momentary thought of digression. “What am I gonna do with you anyway? Nothing! So I don’t guess it really matters, now does it?”

“Thank you. I feel fortunate that you are accepting of my lifestyle and my habits.” His response was nice, but I could tell that he was now slightly dejected.

“Excuse me, I’ll be right back. I need to pee.”

“Okay, so do I.”

I didn’t really have to pee. I just needed a moment to reflect and think. I sat down on my bed and tried my best to not be judgmental, but I couldn’t help myself! I decided not to speak with this person any more. It just didn’t seem right to me. Maybe he was just trying to gain sympathy - or maybe not! Either way, I didn’t think that a 38-year-old married man with this addiction could match any of my interests.

“Welcome back, Iron Angel. Did everything come out alright?”

“No, I didn't go after all.”

“Will you take your phone to the restroom?”

Okay, now things were getting awkward as this conversation was taking a turn in a direction that I really didn’t like.

“Eww, who does that? Why would I do that?”

"Okay, sorry. Go now then."

"Alright, I will. Be right back!"

I contemplated just disconnecting the app and ending the chat, but I realized that I had gotten sucked into the conversation. Curiosity is my downfall sometimes. I took my time and prayed that he would be gone by the time I returned; however, that was not the case. Much to my disappointment, he was still there. I just took more time and grabbed some food from the fridge. Unbelievably, he was still there on hold when I returned!

"Okay, I'm back."

"Welcome back."

Things had gotten awkward for me now, so I fumbled for words to keep the conversation going that I wished had naturally ended. "Did you even wash your hands?"

He responded in a nonchalant tone, "No."

"Eww! I knew it."

My comment triggered a defensive tone from him. "What? I didn't touch it!"

"I can't envision how that is even possible."

I wasn't prepared for his emasculating reply. "I sat, just like you do."

This guy was becoming less of a man by the minute. I always envisioned men standing up to pee. In fact, I see that as a distinguishing characteristic between men and women. I was rapidly becoming more and more disenchanted with this conversation, but somehow, I kept it going. “Well, I still washed my hands.”

“Oh, you must have had to wipe and wash because you got something on your hands? Why don’t you just air dry?”

The urination conversation was really irking me at this point, so I tried to derail it. “Look, I didn't ask for a vivid description of what you did in the bathroom.”

“I didn’t wipe the tip of my penis till the last drop was out.” Apparently, he didn’t get my not-so-subtle hint!

I rolled my eyes at the thought of this guy sitting down to pee and then wiping his tip as well. It was not behavior befitting of the kind of stud I was searching for. “Geeezzzz, shhhh!” I urged.

He tried to soften the mood and make light of the situation with a laugh. “What? I just diggle and dangle!”

“Yuck! So, do you wash hands in any circumstance?”

“I don't wash my hands when I pee because I know where my dick has been. In fact, it might be the cleanest part of my body. If anything, I should wash my hands BEFORE I pee. My hands have touched everything - door knobs, money, you name it…”

"You do have a point. I guess I'll have to go inside a men's restroom to investigate at least once."

"Have you not seen a man pee before?"

"No, but I was talking about to see if they washed their hands - not to watch them pee. Why would I do that? That's disgusting."

"Oh, so you just want to see if men wash their hands? I get it now. So, are you a germaphobe or something?!"

"You are being silly."

I reconsidered my decision to terminate the chat as we both had a good, loud laugh before we continued this stupid conversation. This did secretly provoke me to wonder what percentage of men actually wash their hands after a bathroom visit.

"So, my Iron Angel, are you getting ready to sleep?"

I relaxed a bit and softened my tone, "Yes, under my sheets."

"Well, that sounds cozy."

"Yep, especially considering it's freaking cold!"

"So, what do you sleep in to keep warm - sweater and pj's or nothing at all?"

"Yep, it's tees and pj's for me."

"Nice, do you always sleep in pj's and tees?"

I suddenly felt the urge to be sexy, so I mirrored the tone of my voice to match my mood. "But things come off after a while."

"Really? What comes off after a while?"

"If I am sweating, my pj's or tees or both come off!"

"Oh, okay. If it is warm, do you sleep just in panties with no top? Do you live alone or have a roommate?"

"I live alone."

"That's great for privacy and freedom. I love privacy too. Before I got married, I always lived by myself. I have a question for you. When you have to step out of the bedroom, do you put a T-shirt on or do you walk around the house in panties.

This bad boy voyeur was prying a little too deep now, so I had to derail his line of questioning. "What the hell are panties?

"Um, what do you mean? You don't wear panties at home?"

"Panties are for grannies! Who wears them now?"

He got a little defensive, but even more interested. "Some people still do. So, what do you wear? A thong?"

"Nope. Not my style either. To be honest, I'm feeling awkward having a conversation about panties with you. But if you really must know, I wear hipsters and cross-back sports bras most of the time."

"My apologies for the awkward conversation. I didn't know your feelings about panties."

I sighed, "It's like an all-time low. Of all the things we could be talking about, we're talking about panties."

"I'm sorry. I am learning," he replied in an apologetic tone, but then immediately followed it up with another stupid statement in a sarcastic tone, "I learned today, that I like them!"

"Seriously Adam, I am going to kill you if say anything else about panties." At this point, I was sure that he had found the line and learned not to cross it.

"Nope, you will never hear it from me again! I will officially take off my boxer briefs and T-shirt when I sleep from now on."

"I am curious, where is your better half?"

"Oh, she is messing with something on her laptop - probably shopping or researching something online."

"Is she somewhere near you?"

"Yes."

"And you are chatting with me - with no guilt?"

"Yes, but only with you."

"Have you ever gotten caught in action?"

"I used to feel guilty before I started going to my therapist, but he helped me feel better about the guilt. Luckily, I've never been caught."

"What if she finds out - will that break up your marriage?"

"She already knows about my voyeuring, so I doubt it would break up our marriage."

"Why do you think I am chatting with you? If not for sex, then what do you think my ultimate agenda is?"

Adam took a moment to compose his thoughts and get serious.

"Look, she knows I am hypersexual, so she is okay with the things that I do - as long as I don't ignore her and her needs, she is fine." He paused for a second before answering the second half of my question. "I don't know you, but it seems like you just enjoy the company from chatting online to someone genuine without pretense."

I paused to reflect. There was truth in his last comment that resonated with me. He was right - I found myself just enjoying the conversation and the virtual company of someone. Even a lame conversation with a married man was exciting, considering my alternatives to boredom at the moment.

I was quite pleased with the fact that I was able to accumulate more than 1000 points on this app on my first day. Therefore, the software placed me in Channel 1. It's my understanding that this was a big deal and considered to be exclusive. I guess I was added just in time because the channel lit up with activity. I listened in, as quite a few people were talking and a handful of people even sang or played musical instruments.

With my belly full of food and my soul full of courage, I prepared myself to make a grand entrance into Channel 1. I took a sip of water and confidently broke into the ongoing chatter and music. "Hey everyone!"

Hmmm... a few seconds went by, but no one acknowledged me at all. That was definitely not the response that I was hoping for - especially considering how popular I previously was. Could it be that my popularity was only momentary?

I cleared my throat and suppressed the newly rising lump that had found its way there. Again, I greeted the group with a cheerful, "Hello everyone."

This time I got a response from a few people, but it wasn't overwhelming. I didn't foresee all the males giving me their undivided attention, but I figured I could garner the affection of at least a few more than this. I sensed my nervousness rising as a result of what I considered extreme rejection. And just like that, I received a private channel invite, which I quickly accepted before I made more of a fool of myself on Channel 1.

"Hola, Mr.UW."

His response was prompt and forward, "Hellooooo lady, are you alone?"

"Yes, I live alone. What does UW stand for? I'm curious to know."

Apparently, it was funny - whatever it stood for, because he laughed out loud for a minute too long before answering, "Well, it stands for… I am your___."

I wasn't sure exactly what that meant, but I turned red with anger and shame. I really didn't like having a conversation about underwear. It's not a topic that I envisioned myself having with even a boyfriend or my future husband. I contemplated whether to react at all or just ignore his foolish comment.

My silence must have clued him into the fact that I wasn't amused.

"Are you offended?" he asked.

"Yes."

"We all wear them. How could a simple piece of cloth offend you in any way? How about paper tissue? Does paper tissue offend you?"

Now this guy was clearly just trying to be a jerk - and he was succeeding!

"No," I answered curtly.

"What's that on your head?"

"Can you see me?"

"Of course I can," he laughed.

He had me concerned for a hot minute until I realized he was pulling my leg and trolling me. He was trying to bait me into turning my camera on. We chatted for a few more hours. He turned out to actually be pretty funny and had me laughing my lungs out. I fell asleep sometime around 2 am. I slept well as I was assured that I now had someone to talk to tomorrow.

The next day, I woke up even later in the afternoon. The first thing I did was to login to iVoice. I couldn't wait to learn more about my new friend. I was highly disappointed when I didn't see him on Channel 1, so I brushed my teeth with a heavy heart. I made myself some lunch and kept a close watch on the app to see if he popped into the Channel. I killed time by quietly listening to what other users were talking about. Most of their chatter was nonsense about their promiscuous desires. Only a handful of people were talking about sensical things such as politics, war, education and other topics of relevance. Amidst all the crap, it's worth it to hear a bit of good conversation. I got good at muting out the rest of the chatter. Then finally, Mr. UW popped online!

I eagerly greeted him, "Hi Mr.UW, nice to see you again."

His reply was soul-crushing, "Who are you?"

After a long pause, I replied, “We had a conversation a few hours ago.”

He laughed in the familiar and jovial tone that I remembered from last night. “Did we cyber? Let's do it again, babe.”

I knew it, he really was a jerk. Obviously, the conversation meant more to me than it did to him. I responded innocently, “What is that? And also, don't call me babe - I'm not a pig.”

He laughed at me again and accused me of not having a sense of humor.

Just as I was about to give this guy a piece of my mind, someone named Phantom came rushing into the conversation to defend me.

“Stay away from her,” Phantom demanded.

Mr. UW got instantly defensive. “Oh, is she yours?” he scoffed. “Hang your fishy and lay your claim then!”

“Be gone, loser.” Phantom said.

Just as it seemed Phantom had gotten rid of one pest, another one named Frogy chimed in, “Did you crash him?”

“Yes, I did - and you can join him,” Phantom commanded with confidence in his voice. “Hi Iron Angel, I would like to invite you to leave this scene and join me on a more private channel.”

I accepted his invitation and quickly switched to the other channel. Astonishingly, there were no other users on that channel. I assumed it must be some sort of a private channel. I was relieved to be in private again as I subjected myself to his greetings and welcome. I proceeded to recount my conversation with the jerk from the night before. Phantom explained to me how most users were just looking for cybersex in private chat rooms. Then he made it a point to tell me how he preferred to talk in private over open channels. I concurred with him.

We made small talk for a while, but I was really tired, so I politely brought the conversation to a close. "Hey Phantom, it's my time to sleep, I will catch you tomorrow. I'm going to go to bed," I whispered in a soft tone.

"Well, if you could leave your mic on, it would be an honor for me," he suggested in a hopeful tone.

"Dude, I snore so bad," I giggled.

"I can handle snoring, my night angel."

I could envision him smiling on the other end of the conversation. "At your own risk," I said with a mushy smile of my own.

I realized that I didn't really know much about myself before I began using this app. I was quickly discovering that this online venture was turning into an introspective journey. I had no idea that I could talk or giggle so much with a complete stranger!

The drawback to my late night chatting was that waking up late was beginning to become a regular habit; however, my morning turned out to be unusually pleasant as I received an unexpected wakeup call.

"Hey sugar, good morning! Did you sleep well?" His voice sounded as fresh as a fruit.

"Oh, you're still there? I didn't notice," I answered as I folded some blankets. "Hey, I will catch you in a while," I said as I quickly put the phone down. I needed to answer nature's call first and I danced my way to the restroom. I relieved myself as I thought about how I could overcome the opposing high of an adrenaline rush and conversely, the low of exhaustion from lack of sleep.

I hopped across the floor to the kitchen. My heart was pounding. I could only think about what I should stuff my growling stomach with. I eat like a pig, but I look like a skinny giraffe. I quickly arrived at the conclusion that there was nothing at home that was going to satisfy my hunger. I dreaded leaving home though, because driving in the harsh, cold wind was taxing and downright uncomfortable. I then had a revelation and thought of the perfect solution. I ordered pizza delivery!

The pizza arrived in no time and as I began to eat, I followed my suspicion and checked iVoice. My suspicion was right - Phantom was still there!

"Oh my, Jesus - you're still here!" My consciousness returned to me as I satisfied my prevailing hunger with another slice of pizza.

"Of course I am," he enthusiastically replied. "Are you still in your pajamas? Lazy bum!"

"No, I am not. I'm wearing shorts."

"Short or long shorts?"

"Decently short, I guess. They still qualify as 'shorts', not 'longs'!" I sarcastically answered.

"Please don't tell me that they are black, Victoria's Secret shorts."

"You are damn right, they are!"

"Dear God, what have I gotten myself into?"

"Does my Victoria's Secret preference bother you?"

"Nah, it's just not what I want to see on my girl."

"Well considering I am NOT your girl, I have the freedom to wear whatever I please."

He disregarded my statement and redirected the conversation, but stayed on the same topic. "What color do you normally wear?"

"Let me see... red, pink, blue, lavender and so many more."

"You are bold." His compliment was followed up by another question, "Makeup or no makeup?"

"Ewwww, who wears that? It's for grandmas who hide crevices and highways on their bony faces."

"Could you say that again?"

I paused for a second for emphasis before responding, "What, granny? Highway? Or what didn't you get?"

"No, say 'ewww' - I want to record you and save that for later."

"Wait, what? How can you save it for later?" I was perplexed.

"This app allows us to save 60 seconds of audio each day. Today, I choose to use my 60 seconds to capture your voice saying 'ewww'."

And now I was vexed to learn that my voice could potentially be recorded without my permission or awareness, but I still had a bigger concern. "Hey Phantom, can you see me?"

"No and yes. Ethically no, technically yes. There is some software available that will allow you to remotely turn on someone's camera - or keep you logged into a channel, or even find your phone number."

"How can I save myself from such a breach?" I wondered what someone could actually find out about me. After all, I lived a pretty quiet and guarded life.

Phantom tried to play coy and bargain with me. "What's in it for me if I tell you the ultimate solution? A kiss? A date?"

I was flattered, but I wasn't about to let him know it. "Ewww… What's next, a marriage proposal?"

"Fair enough, let's settle down with a kiss first."

"Ewww."

I must have humbled him a little with my rejection because he sounded a little dejected.

"Whatever, I got what I needed. I have your expression saved. So, I guess I'll go ahead and tell you the solution." He baited my anticipation with his hesitation. "Just stick some duct tape over your webcam. That will do the trick."

We laughed hysterically and called it a night, ending the chat on a humorous note. I couldn't help but wonder about the duct tape trick and whether it was really necessary, or if he was just pulling my leg.

CHAPTER TWO

Temptation

I awoke the next morning elated from my conversation with Phantom the previous night. As I was getting ready for work, I checked my phone a couple of times to see if he was online. I tried my best not to be overzealous, but I just couldn't stop my emotions from running wild.

My car was still at the studio so I hailed a cab, and as I rode through the downtown traffic, thoughts from the previous night's conversation replayed in my head. Phantom really impressed me by how he jumped in to save the day. He has a certain sense of humor that delights me as well. Not to mention that the duct tape was a great idea. I certainly would have never thought of it! He seems to be so tech savvy and certainly knows more about computers than I do. I wondered if he was in the IT or technology industry.

My workday at the art gallery breezed by. In between a few daydreams, I watched my employee, Mrs. Martha, slowly walking through the gallery to attend to potential buyers. She is such an adorable old lady and I'm very blessed to have her work for me. I returned to my office every now and then to check if Phantom was online or if he had left a text message. After lunch, I decided to disassociate myself from the thought of being with Phantom and completely focus on work for the rest of my day. After all, I had things to get done and focusing all of my thoughts and attention on this new online affection wasn't going to allow me to be productive at work. I smiled, sighed and went about my business as usual.

When I got home, I settled for the unconditional and always available affection from Maggy, my cute little German Shepherd and Lab mix puppy. She was pouncing on me and bubbling over with joy that I was finally home. She repeated this daily ritual no matter how long I was gone. Ahhh… if only getting affection from the right man could be so easy! I wish I could adopt the perfect guy from the same rescue center where I got Maggy.

As my dinner of noodles and veggies boiled on the stove, I got the premonition to check in with Dorothy to make sure she was okay. I hadn't heard from her since I left the party, so I wanted to make sure that she was safe and hadn't killed herself with sex, drugs or alcohol. My focus was interrupted and I forgot about Dorothy, because when I picked up my phone, I saw a text from Phantom.

"Come here," was the only thing he said.

I was surprised by such a text. I didn't understand the context or the odd nature of his request.

"Okayyyyy! What's going on?" I quickly replied.

"What are you doing?"

"Just cooking dinner. Would you like something too?" I offered in jest.

"Pick the phone up so that we can talk."

"Okayyyy! You are scaring me." I picked up the phone and dialed into the chat to find out why he was being so demanding.

I was relieved that his voice was the familiar, comforting tone that I had been longing for all day, rather than the harsh demeanor and demanding tone of his texts. So much can be lost in translation with text conversations.

"I want you to go stand against the wall and hold your phone up," he said in a seductive tone.

"Okay, I just did. Now what?"

I heard him take a drag off his cigarette and then exhale. I imagined his breath blowing on my neck rather than puffing smoke into the air.

"Close your eyes. Imagine my hands on your waist and my bare body pressing you against the wall. Can you vividly picture that? I want you to feel my strength overcome you. Now I'm going to slide my fingers through your hair and push it to one side and then tuck it behind your ear for a moment, before I grab it and pull at it gently. I embrace you with my other arm and pull your waist closer and tighter to mine as I pull your head back by your hair with my other hand. How do you like that? How does it make you feel?"

I was momentarily lost in ecstasy. I snapped back to reality and cleared my throat before answering, “Sorry, I wasn’t listening. I was fixing my head set. What did you say?”

He found it hard to believe that I had disengaged from the conversation at such an important moment. “You are some girl!” he laughed.

“I was just kidding. I have to confess, I did hear what you said to me. I was just having some fun with ya!”

“Huh, so do you really want to have some fun with me?”

I innocently said, “Yes,” but I guess I wasn’t convincing enough.

“Are you SURE?”

“Yes, try me,” I responded in a more certain tone.

“What are you thinking of right now?”

“Nothing,” I said in a semi-stunned tone. He put me on the spot, but I was blank - no words came to mind to describe what I was thinking at the time. I didn’t know how to process his inquiry or how to react and answer. I considered just ending my chat with him for good. I felt like he was testing me or trying to judge me as to whether or not I was into such things. Conversely, I realized that I might be judging him right then as well - whether or not he was into such things. I debated with myself for a moment and rationalized whether I should not assume things about him, rather give him a chance and get to know him better. Nonetheless, I decided to end the night's conversation with a polite "goodbye and goodnight".

I awoke the next day with Phantom on my mind and I quickly discovered that what you think about, you bring about. Almost as if he was watching me, he voice messaged me on the app.

"What are you plans for today?" he asked.

Delighted to hear from him so promptly (especially considering my abrupt exit from the previous night's conversation), I contained my excitement so as not to seem overzealous.

"Ah, nothing much. I'm about to make myself something to eat and then take a shower."

"Okay, can you do something for me?" he asked with a certain degree of mischief in his voice.

I giggled and innocently replied, "Yes, what? Do you want me to make you blueberry pancakes and be your mommy?"

His demeanor became even more serious, yet still very mischievous, "I want you to move your lazy bum and go fill the tub."

I blushed, but reveled at the thought of a nice bath. "Gosh, you get me worked up. Fine, I will fill the tub with water. What next?" Instead, I turned the water on in the kitchen sink and washed a couple of dirty dishes that I needed to cook with.

"What are you wearing?"

I hesitated and surveyed my body for a moment to acquaint myself with what I was actually wearing. I debated whether or not to be honest or fabricate something. "Ah, hmmmm!"

"Don't be shy, you can tell me," he coaxed in a seductive voice.

"Okay. I just get a little nervous with such things. It's tough for me to express myself. I often have difficulty sharing my emotions, state of mind, or feelings," I said as I pulled the cutting board from a drawer and then fetched a knife from a different drawer.

"Let me help you. You can start by taking off your clothes one by one and as you do, just say what you are doing." His tone was reassuring and alluring.

Here we go again. This kind of thing had been happening over and over again. He would start off with a normal conversation, but quickly digress into something sensual. I have been very vocal about the fact that I don't enjoy this type of conversation and that I don't 'do myself' over the phone. It's just so lame! I wondered if maybe I wasn't using the right words or tone to make myself clear on this point. I think, at times I feared that I wouldn't have enough attention from these men if I chose not to entertain them in such a manner; however, I shouldn't need such company or friends or 'friends with benefits' who talk about sex 24/7. When it's not working out for me, I try to completely call it quits, but these men change their strategies - they apologize, they beg for forgiveness, they ask me to take some time off, cool my temper and so on and so forth. My decision on this subject would remain the same today or tomorrow or a decade later. Some men believe that they can bring change in me, but they fail to understand that I have been conditioned in such a fashion for the last three decades. It would take another three decades for them to change me. I was certain that none of these men possessed such perseverance.

They had respect for me and for who I am as a person, but they all want to get in my pants for the same reason. I usually don't experiment with my morality and I am completely firm on how I want to conduct myself, but for once I thought maybe I would move forward, in spite of my own boundaries, just to see how low he could go. What more could he do or say? Would he start to handle himself while on the phone? I would hate to see myself as someone's toy, but it would give me some clarity regarding his final agenda and whether his motive was to have someone help him release over phone. I was sure that was the case, but I still went ahead for confirmation on both ends. I would have something substantial to debate with him, that would be his own words. If I stopped and had a confrontation now, he would deny all his promiscuous intentions.

"Okay. I think I can do that," I said as I fumbled through the fridge to grab a few items. "I am wearing a button up long sleeve shirt. I will have to undo three buttons to slide this shirt off…button one, button two, button three…and now it's on the floor..." and by on the floor, I was referring to the clove of garlic I had just dropped, but I continued with my seductive white lie. "I have a black t-shirt on under it that I'm now sliding up and over my head. Now that t-shirt is on the floor with my button-up. So I'm just standing here in my black hipster underwear now. The tub is almost full and I am gonna slide the hipsters down my smoothly shaven legs before I settle down into the steamy tub." The tub wasn't full, but the kitchen sink was about to overflow because I had left the water running without hitting the garbage disposal to clear the drain as to not foil my erotic narrative with the familiar noise. In my silliest voice, I relayed my next move. "Oops, my hipsters are around my ankles now. I just stepped my left foot out and then kicked them across the room with my right foot. They flew through the air and landed on my head." In actuality, a cherry tomato that I had just sliced into, shot its juice skyward and I felt it nest in my hair.

I could tell that Phantom was getting aroused as the tone in his voice cracked for one second when he spoke again.

"You are turning me on so much. I am all loaded and ready to shoot."

I hit my limit and redirected the conversation. "Um, can we change the topic? I'm not comfortable with where this is going." I scraped some chopped veggies into an iron skillet.

"Sure. Tell me about the tub - did you put something in it - bubbles?"

"Yes, it's all bubbly!" I laughed to myself as the skillet sizzled with oil, onion and garlic.

"Now take a picture of your legs and send it to me."

Wow, the change of topic didn't last long before he redirected it back to something sexual.

I paused before inquiring, "Are you serious? Why?"

Seductively, he reasoned with me, "I just wanna see you that way. I can't ask you for a webcam session, so a picture of your legs will suffice nicely."

I ran into the bathroom for proper effect and I snapped a few pics of my legs from my lower thighs down to my toes. I deliberated for a minute or two and then reluctantly pushed the send button to share the images with him.

Once he received the pictures, he was appreciative, but eager to wrap the conversation up quickly. He said goodbye and told me that he would be back in a few hours because he was headed out of town for some work. He got to see my legs and I got to cook in peace. I did, however, promise myself a rain check on soaking in a warm, bubbly bath later.

Later that night, we caught up online again. He found me on Channel 1 and ordered me to log off of the group chat.

There was a deep silence before I heard him light a cigarette. I could hear him taking deep, constant puffs. I wondered what he was thinking. I just didn't want him to be upset. Frankly, I was just having a fun conversation in the main chatroom, but he was not completely convinced that I didn't intend to ignore him. I hadn't talked to him for an hour or so, and now, all of a sudden, he decided to start acting like a possessive, jealous boyfriend. He raised his voice at me, demanding me to not speak with any other users on iVoice.

Phantom told me how older men lured young, naive girls to do things on the internet that they wouldn't normally do in private, let alone in public. Then these predators would post their altered clips on pornography sites. Phantom spoke of a software named "Hide Me". Once downloaded, it automatically allows the user to make necessary changes to other people's webcam driver so that it never sleeps. There was another distinctive program which allows users to save and record all conversations day in and day out. Perverts can then upload these voice recordings on a site called iTube.

As he talked and warned of these dangers, I did some browsing and soon found some recordings on iTube, just as he had mentioned. I found a channel 9 iTube audio where two men and a woman were disclosing identities of other users.

Phantom warned me over and over to stay away from a guy called Cobra. According to Phantom, Cobra chose to play the bad guy and punish everyone for no apparent reason. Supposedly he recorded over 150 clips of women with no clothes on. He just so happened to be the co-owner of a porn website that featured cam pranks and posted personal details of users.

Things were getting sketchy, but I trusted Phantom and I felt like he was looking out for me.

"Hey Phantom, if you don't mind me asking, why are you telling me all of this and being so protective of me? We just met online - why do you care?"

"Well honestly, I have been observing you in Channel 1. You come across as a genuine, simple, modest, and sensitive person. I wouldn't want you to get hurt. I won't let that happen to you, as long as I am alive."

I hummed a deep "Hmmm…" and paused to collect my thoughts. "I don't know what to say. But thanks - and yes, you are right, I am super sensitive and I am getting to know more about this online chat world. I don't understand why people don't understand that I am not like all of the others in here, I'm just not totally interested in having sex talks day in and day out. I think that's all people want in here."

"This place is not for you. You should quit if such things bother you."

I agreed with him to myself, but I responded differently. "It doesn't bother me too much because I choose to block such users; however, I am somewhat disappointed that no one actually cares more about a person than simply sexting or 'cybering' with them."

"I care about you," he said.

I appreciated his sentiment, but I didn’t share my appreciation - instead, I threw out my dismissive response and tone. “Yeah, yeah,” I chided.

I decided to call it a night and hang up the phone before it got too mushy.

The next night we caught up again. Although the conversation started off in a serious tone, I quickly jumped out of bed and migrated to the couch. I began twirling my hair as my mood lightened.

In a low sexy voice, Phantom said, "I wanna say something. Is this the best time to talk?"

I guess I already knew by this time what he wanted to say. Hesitantly, I replied, “Sure, shoot." I immediately realized that my choice of words was poor.

“Shoot, huh? Baby, do you want me to shoot in you or on you?”

I decided to respond in a disgusted tone, “Ewww man, what the heck!”

He chuckled before he knocked me down a notch. "Look, you are not the first girl in my life. Many have come and gone. But I must say, you bring out the best in me. I think I am in love with you."

And then there was a long awkward pause.

I waited until he finally broke the silence again. "You don't like me?"

I laughed fanatically. "I don't have time for all this crap. This is not what I am looking for. I actually have good options in the real world. I don't want an imaginary boyfriend online. Period!"

His reply was direct and to the point, and his tone was genuine. “Do you want me?” he asked as he exhaled heavily from what I could only assume was a drag off of a cigarette.

I paused to reflect on his curt and direct question. Before responding, I composed myself and answered his question with the same question, but in an insisting tone.

“Do you want me?”

Without hesitation he answered, “I want you right now and right here in my arms with me. I will do more to you than you can imagine.”

I didn’t know how to respond. In one way, it was what I wanted to hear, but in other ways, I was frightened. My heart skipped a few beats as I responded, “You scare me when you say this.”

“It’s okay to be scared. I will question you one last time. Do you want me?”

I answered his question with a question of my own. “Will you leave me?”

I thought he said he was only going to ask me one more time… last time, but he persisted, “Do you want me?”

And then I responded with another question. "Will you ever think of me after this?"

Yet again, he demanded, "Do you want me?"

I finally decided to get serious. "Look, I like you a lot."

I had danced around his question long enough and it became apparent as his demeanor changed to a more demanding and even slightly angered tone.

"DO YOU WANT ME?" he shouted into the phone.

I finally reached my limit. "No. I don't want you. But I may want you - just give me some time."

My last sentence didn't go through because I could hear white silence on the other end of the phone. What an inopportune time for the app to disconnect. Disappointed in myself, I put my phone down and looked at his profile status, just in time to see him go offline. I quickly logged out of the app and logged in again to see if anything had changed. Sadly, that didn't work - nothing had changed. Feverishly, I logged in again and again and again - each time hoping he would come back. I soon began to believe that he was trying to teach me a lesson.

I waited for five minutes, then fifteen and then an hour slowly went by. It was half past 2 AM and I could no longer keep my eyes open. I had a sinking feeling in my soul. I couldn't forgive myself for breaking his heart. I wish I would have just said "yes" and then come up with a logical explanation later in time. All he wanted was a yes from me - yes, that I wanted him in my life. He didn't ask me to make babies with him or even meet him tomorrow for a date. He just wanted to know if I wanted him in my life.

How stupid and stubborn could I possibly be? Or maybe this was an indication that we couldn't be together as we are both stubborn and would simply end up breaking each other's hearts. I was just so scared of his promiscuity. Maybe sex is all he can talk about over the phone. Maybe in actuality, he doesn't have the guts to please a girl in his actual life. Or maybe, there is that chance that he is just so ugly that no one wants to sleep with him. Or maybe he is HIV positive. My mind ran wild with possibilities before I finally stopped and questioned myself as to why I was subjecting myself to this kind of torture from a person that I didn't know anything about. After all, the only thing he had done in these last few days was to dig into my skin and talk about my hair and what not. I had to ask myself if this was what I really wanted in my life.

I checked my phone and logged into the app again. My heart was racing and my palms were sweating. I had this deep, stabbing and twisting feeling inside my tummy.

Why the hell should I care about him, if he doesn't give a damn about how I am feeling? Does he even understand how much guilt I am going through right now - and did he inflict it on purpose? Why can't he respect my opinion and the fact that I'm just not into cybersex. He needs to put a leash on his desires and not kill our newfound friendship.

I changed my attitude and made up my mind that it's a new day and a fresh beginning. I decided that I was no longer stopping for anything or anyone. I resolved to just live my life the way I wanted to. I logged back into the app and used my accumulated points to get into Channel 1. I didn't care one bit if this Cobra guy that he kept warning me about was on the channel, I was going to do my thing and stop waiting for Phantom to come back.

I simply went on without him and interacted with everyone on the channel. The other users were highly interested in me and had lots of questions to ask. I loved all the attention I was getting again. Regardless of whether they were male or female, everyone was going gaga over my voice. It felt great to be wanted and to intrigue strangers simply with my voice. I loved the attention, but I longed to speak to Phantom again.

A few days passed and every day I thought of him, constantly hoping he would get back to me so that I could be able to explain myself. Every morning, the first thing I did was send him a message. I got the same notification each time - the disheartening, automatic message said that the user had blocked me. At nights before going to bed, I messaged him again - and again I got the same message.

Sunday was the fourth day since I had last spoken to him, but I finally saw him online; however, he was not on any channel. I waited and waited and waited. I patiently waited all day before I decided to just go ahead and kill my ego and send him an e-gift with a note attached (fortunately, the app still let you spend your points to send a gift, even when you are blocked). Bingo, it worked! He replied almost instantly after I hit the send button.

“Hey, how are you?” he nonchalantly asked.

“Are you done being mad at me?”

“Sweetheart, I am not mad at you.”

His voice sounded sincere, but I had serious doubts as to his honesty with me.

“What is going on? Why did you block me?”

“I didn’t block you.”

I swallowed my pride and humbled my voice. “Honestly, please let me say what I have to say.”

“Okay, I am here and waiting,” he said in an almost annoyed tone.

“What I was trying to say is let's get to know each other better. I don't know what you do or where you are. Plus, I can't say I want you just for the heck of it.”

“Why not?” he practically begged.

“You know what I mean,” I reasoned.

“Look, you know the worst side of me. And if you want me back, I am sure you will fall in love with the good part of me.”

"I don't know how I can possibly commit in just a few days of knowing you."

"What do you want to know about me?"

I thought for a moment. "Let's start with what you do to earn a living."

"Fair enough. I am an investment broker and I worked as an investment banker for five years. I was not growing very much in my career, so I made the decision to go solo."

"How about family?"

"I have an aunt and a niece. That's my family."

I continued grilling him with rapid-fire questions. "What is your real agenda here?"

Without hesitation he answered, "I want a soul mate."

I wasn't buying it and I replied accordingly, "See, I don't understand that. Why don't you look for a soul mate outside of the virtual world? People can hide behind a screen and say whatever they want online."

"I have had a few relationships outside of this app. None of them worked out for various reasons. In fact, I was dating a girl for a few months and she fucked me - both physically and mentally too. I am not the naive, guy next door type that you might think I am. I'm still coping with my heartache and I am not ready to go out and do it all over again. But you probably don't want to hear about all of that."

He baited the hook and I bit, giving him permission to share his story with me. He took a toke on his smoke, exhaled and then let me peek into his world a little bit more.

"So I collected a shitload of Pokemon cards when I was younger. And by 'collected', I mean some of them I may or may not have stolen from my schoolmates' book bags. I would then sell these ridiculous cards to kids from other schools for a ridiculous price. Shit, by the time I was seventeen I had probably already made three grand from this, my first foray into 'business'. At eighteen, I was all-in on trading cards and other stuff too. I always knew I'd be good at business. It was this belief that propelled me to graduate from a top business school and ultimately walk straight into my own personal office space at The World Trade Center as an investment banker. I was so glad that I made the decision to evolve from simply trading cards and other commodities to making a positive impact in the finance business. Because this is when, where and how I met the love of my life."

I listened intently as Phantom shed some light on his past. I was intrigued and eager to learn more about him. I didn't care that I was about to hear about the love of his life. I just wanted to know him.

He continued, "She was a model in New York and was working for a reputable agency when I met her. We hit it off quickly and moved in to a very nice penthouse and spent a wonderful year together, until I caught her with another man."

He paused a moment to take a drag on his cigarette. I could tell that he was still hurting from this heartbreak.

"She tried to justify her actions with some twisted rationale that she felt trapped in our relationship." He sighed, "Yeah, if living in an awesome penthouse with a guy who loves you and takes care of you and asks very little in return is being 'trapped', then I guess she was right. I trapped her."

Again, I heard the familiar deep inhale and exhale of a cigarette drag during his dramatic moment of silence.

"The real truth is that she got into some trouble online and this guy blackmailed her into sleeping with other men - or else he would post her pics publicly online. So she said. So, that's a little bit about my past. I don't really want to elaborate more at this time as I choose to focus on the present and not live in the past. Now I have a question for you - are we ready to take it to the next level?"

I waited a moment before responding. I was still processing the history he had shared with me. I had a feeling I knew what the answer was, but I probed anyway, "What is the next level - a date, sex?"

"Nothing. Never mind," he said in a frustrated tone.

"What?"

"I just opened up to you and shared a secret about my past. Don't you wanna see me and find out how I look?"

"I'm sorry, but it doesn't really matter much to me. Eventually we all will grow old and bald." I thought my comment would make him feel better and change the course of the conversation, but he still persisted along the same line of questioning.

"What do you want?"

I didn't have to think long because I answered truthfully and swiftly, "I don't know."

He hesitated and inhaled a drag before throwing out an interesting suggestion.

"Okay, let's do this... We will go on three e-dates. Maybe that will help you figure out what you really want. After the last date, you will have an additional two days to make up your mind whether you want me or not. But, when I get back to you, I will need a firm answer. Fair enough?"

I figured what could be the harm in three e-dates. His proposal sounded good, so I accepted.

I rolled over in bed just in time to see the first rays of sunlight pierce through the slats of the blinds on my window. I knew it was going to be the beginning of a beautiful day. I dialed into the app and Phantom immediately connected with me. We literally talked all day. I just couldn't get enough conversation with him. He made me laugh constantly with his bag of silly jokes.

In between his jokes, was sincere conversation about his aunt and niece - and even his assistant at work. I was really enjoying getting to know him, yet I still held back personal and sensitive emotions of my own. I figured they were better left unsaid for the time being.

He is certainly smart, witty and sarcastic, but rarely too sensitive. I really enjoyed almost all of our conversations - except the times when he insisted on role play. That made me really nervous and I'm still not sure if I even enjoyed it or not. I think my body enjoyed it because I got dripping wet every time he initiates the role play. In fact, I find myself dripping wet pretty much most of the time lately when I think of him. I often have to change multiple times a day.

"Did you use your bed in a better way?" he asked in his sultry voice.

"What does that even mean?"

"I thought you were going to take a nap and I figured you would pamper yourself a little in bed."

"Well, I didn't. I took a run instead."

"Well good for you, but you don't have to be such a shy girl… it's cold outside. You should make your body warm now after your run..."

I took a deep breath and mustered up some courage before I shared some intimate thoughts. "I will be real honest - I can't stop getting moist between my legs - like all day. My mind and body are dominated by sexual desires."

"Wow, that's what a guy needs in a girl. I guarantee that you wouldn't be able to handle me all night."

Not to be outdone, I said, "Try me!"

"Whatever. After three or four orgasms, you would beg me to stop."

I was determined to win this verbal battle of physical prowess. "Try me! That's all I can say."

"I would make you super wet when you are driving, your thighs would be soaked." He paused to take a drag off his cigarette. As he exhaled, he said, "I don't know how much you cum, but I would make you climax after I turn you around and enter you from behind."

"You have no clue about me." I tried to play coy.

"Would you sit on my face and let me eat you until you gush?"

My coyness was defeated as I admitted, "Absolutely!"

"I will make your tits so bouncy. You would beg for me to stop."

My heart was pounding, my pulse was racing and my juices were flowing, but my mind came back to its senses. I knew I had to end this before lust overcame me.

"Why are we having this conversation? I feel off. There's no emotion. No love, just lust."

"Because you are on fire. You don't know me - yet!"

"I tend to ignore these desires and listen to my brain."

"Look, what is that one thing that would make you crazy?"

I pondered his question for a minute. "Knowing me." I paused to let those two words sink in for a minute before I explained, "For someone to know me like I know myself - all of me - my moods, my mind, my body. For someone to be able to read me and know me."

"Nice, but what's that one thing that just makes you shiver?" he insisted.

"Hmmmmm… I'm really not sure. Let me think…"

"Well damn, I had you pegged as the type of person that would be very sure of what they wanted."

"Well, it's not just one thing that I can point to. You tell me one and I will follow you. Start with one."

"Okay, here you go...I love it when a girl sits on top of me and grinds her pussy on me. And by on top of me… I mean my face. I want to feel her juices on my lips and ultimately on my chin as she cums, while I nibble on her clit. I want her scent to delight my nose as well. I love pussy - the taste, the smell and the feel of it."

I couldn't resist the urge to be sarcastic with him. "Oh yeah, I don't think you've actually ever done that," I teased.

"I have," he answered emphatically.

"Okay wait. Let me speak. My turn." I tried to calm the arousal in my voice, but it was pointless. "Lay me on my back and then thrust your member into me and dig it in." I cooed a little for additional effect. I was new to this, but I was liking it and it felt natural. "Okay, you are standing and digging in. My legs are on you or up in the air. That position hits the right place inside of me - plus, you can sustain for a long time like this."

I could tell from the energy in his voice that he was enjoying my fantasy as he said, "Oh yeah baby! I am sure you like my balls slapping on your ass. Oh, I can feel it. And I'm holding your legs in the air. Tell me what you want. Tell me what gives you an orgasm, baby!"

His voice pitch and tempo increased in accordance with his obvious arousal (which I promptly derailed).

"On the other hand, I don't mind going down on a guy, but there's no going south on me." Before he could express his disappointment, I continued, "Wait. Would you like to try 77?"

"What the fuck is 77? Tell me about it."

"Okay, so the guy and the girl lay down side by side and bend as the guy spoons the girl from behind. It looks like two 7's. It's like doggy style on your side, laying down."

He reciprocated with another fantasy of his own. "I love keeping it in - even after cumming. Then just lying there, nuzzling your neck. Then, after a few minutes of post-coital bliss, I make you feel my cock swell back up inside you." He was proud of this fantasy. I could tell by the confident tone of his voice. "Would you like me to pound you hard and then slow down? Or keep the pace fast?"

"I like the idea of you growing inside me and I like a mix of both hard and fast as well as smooth and slow, but I don't want to feel like I'm in a hardcore porn movie."

"I love it when it grows inside of you and swells to its maximum. I want you to feel it stretch the inside of your pussy walls. Do you like to play with your clit while my dick is inside of you? Do you want me to kiss your neck while I'm thrusting into you?"

"Actually, I will make you play with my clit. I would take your hand and roll it over my clit, real slow and real smooth," I said as I let out a sensual sigh.

"I would part your lips and touch the soft skin around your vagina as I tease you and make the juices flow out of you. Do you like your tits to be nibbled on? Do you moan loudly?"

"That's how I like my orgasms to happen - with you shoving it in and playing with my clit. Yes, I do like nibbling and even more than that, I enjoy a little pain." I pursed my lips and inhaled heavily to mimic a good pain reaction. "Nope, I don't moan on orgasm, I get very quiet actually. But otherwise during the action, I moan a lot."

"Would you like to be spanked?"

"Oh yes! I've been a bad girl!"

"Shall I spank you on your butt, your clit, or both?"

"Yes, both please! I will ask for that, especially while in the 77 position. Pull my hair back and spank my butt and ride it. Gently though. No aggressive pulling - just hold my hair tight. I like it when the guy feels my butt or spanks my butt while he's behind me."

"How about spanking your clit with my dick?"

"No. I hate that. The reason being that I have no patience when I am that turned on. I am like, it has to be inside me right now."

"No teasing. Got it. How about biting and nibbling? I love slow and tender love bites on a wet pussy before I slide inside with a jerk and wait until it swells to its full potential."

"Okay, I think it's time that I warned you. I bite. And I have a habit of digging my fingernails into guys' backs. I will also bite your lip while we are kissing, if the right stroke is going on."

"How wet are you right now?"

"I reserve my comments and plead the fifth."

"WOW. You go girl! I will replace my fingers with my dick and pump you hard. With every thrust, you bite me harder and harder. Are you wet now? Come on, you must be wet. Smell it. Just take your bottoms off and keep it bare. Feel it for me once, will you? Feel the wetness soaking your inner thighs."

"Please don't take this as rude, but I've got to go."

With urgency in his voice he said, "No wait. Put your finger inside..."

"Nope. I am leaving," I said as I finally squirted. And by squirted, I mean the last bit of Windex onto the bathroom mirror that I had been cleaning all along. "Don't you understand a 'no'? I am not doing any of it. All of this was a big mistake. I am not into such things. I was trying to see how far you would go, but you disappointed me. Either you know nothing about me or you don't care about how I feel about such things. That is all."

And on that note, I hung up.

On our next call, he acknowledged how I felt about the nature of his conversations, apologized and then asked,

"Do you wanna get back to the three dates we talked about?"

I considered this his last chance. He had already proposed this before. Just do it already.

Hesitantly, I replied "Hmmm... okayyyyy..."

I laid it out in such a way that he was smart enough to read the unsaid. I was sure he would come up with a good plan. So I relented and agreed to accept his offer of our first e-date.

On our first e-date, he invited me to a music channel and instructed me to sit patiently and to not say anything or respond in any way. Then he began playing all of my favorite songs! How did he know? Trust me when I say that I'm certain those songs couldn't be on his normal playlist. As I was getting into the music and the fact that he somehow knew all of my favorite songs, he sent me a text.

"Listen to this. I like this one."

I instinctively cocked my head to the side like a puppy dog and said, "Okay, I am listening."

He was playing a song from a 1968 movie 'Sweet November' - after which, he invited me to a private session where he dropped a link in our comment box. I clicked the link and it opened a pop-up window which started playing the movie. It's so cool that we both could watch it in real time. He paused the movie at exactly the 2:50 minute mark for me to settle down and get some food for myself. I was familiar with the movie as I had watched the new version of the same movie, starring Keanu Reeves and Charlize Theron. We ended up watching the entire movie - and I loved it! Then he gave me a virtual kiss goodnight!

I found myself running around the gallery all giddy and acting like a teenager in love.

Mrs. Martha couldn't help but notice the difference in my attitude, so she asked, "Your cheeks are pink - what are you up to dear? Is it a boy that's making you blush all day long?"

I just blushed and smiled, no other response was necessary. She was right and she knew it. No further confirmation was needed. I could feel butterflies in my stomach and the thought of spending time with him got me through the boring workday. I started to notice some changes in me; I smiled a lot more than normal, I bit my lower lip at times and even started biting my nails. It was all strange behavior for me.

The next night was our second e-date and I couldn't wait to see what he would do to top the first date. He didn't disappoint. I was blown away as he invited me to a room with a bunch of nerds who were hosting a trivia game. Who knew it could be so much fun? I really got into the action and found myself throwing out states and their capital cities, rivers, movie titles and many other facts that I didn't even know that I knew! It was fun, educational, original and romantic (in a nerdy sort of way).

He saved our third e-date for Sunday because he knew that my art gallery was open six days a week and that I would have no work on Sunday. He wanted to pick a day where I could forget about work altogether. He was aware that since my father's sudden and untimely death, I was responsible for everything from sales to management to event planning and all the logistics at the gallery. I had shared with him how I was still learning to run the business under the tutelage of Mrs. Martha. I was so fortunate that she was there to help me through it. She had been with my dad since he opened his first show at his first gallery, working by his side as his personal assistant. She was instrumental in helping him start and grow the business and now she was here again in a very instrumental way, humbly helping me keep the business afloat during these tough times. We lost a few big buyers and suppliers - and that was tough. We also had to provide a very high level of security and oftentimes, discretion and anonymity for our bidders and buyers as well. I wasn't experienced enough to handle it all.

The memories however, I handled very well. This very gallery has a vault that opens directly into my dad's former office. I have fond memories of sneaking into the vault to look at the auction paintings, sculptures, jewelry, and books. I missed my father dearly and reveled in the thoughts of good times of the past. But the past had passed and my father was gone, now I could only make new memories in the present.

"Come here," Phantom beckoned with a seductive tone in his voice.

I understood what he meant and I obliged right away.

He played the song ‘Ain't no Sunshine When She is Gone’ and then he used all of his accumulated points to shower me with e-gifts.

“So, do you want to know something about me? Is there anything important that you would like to learn before we moved forward?”

I responded to him with two questions, “First, what do you want to know about my past? And second, why did you choose to play music and trivia on our dates?”

He answered my first question in a rather intimidating manner, “I know everything about you that I need to know.” Then in an effort to seem less like a creep, he went on to elaborate, “By looking at your display picture of a grand piano, I can only assume that it’s yours and that you love music or maybe even play classical music yourself.” Okay, creep status averted. I rotate my profile picture so frequently that I had forgotten I put up the piano. He continued, “I see you as a very smart and intelligent business woman, so I thought putting you in some sort of gaming session would be a great thing to do.” He paused and gave me a moment to reflect on the fact that he was right, before he redirected the questions back at me. “Is that all you wanna know? Nothing about MY past life?”

I could have cared less about his past at the moment. I was fully present in the moment and well aware of the fact that I was now sitting in a puddle. “I wasn't part of your past, plus I can't change it. What good would it do me to know the details of it. Sometimes the past is better left in the past, but if it helps in shaping the future, I would be highly interested to know more about it."

There was a long silence as I waited for Phantom to say something. I only heard him taking drags off of his cigarette and exhaling into the phone. I let this go on for a few minutes (which seemed like an eternity) before I finally hung up and terminated the call. I got the impression he wanted to let me in on his past, but I didn't trust it to be an honest snapshot anyway. I felt like there was more behind the curtain.

Meanwhile, as the phone went silent and the connection terminated, Phantom methodically twirled the lit end of his cigarette butt into the ashtray to extinguish it as he exhaled a mouthful of smoke into the air. He thought to himself, 'I can't believe she doesn't want to know about me. She has no idea - no idea who I am and what I've done. If only she knew...'

His jaw clenched and his brow furrowed as he winced and then calmly placed the phone down on the table. He hoped that she would make the right decision after taking a few days to think about it.

CHAPTER THREE

Phantom Unmasked

I paced the room and chain smoked a few cigarettes. 'Does my past help shape my future?' I pondered her question all night after the abrupt end to our conversation. The statement had moved me to a direction that I choose not to go very often.

My phone rang and I reached for it, hoping for it to be her, but that was not the case.

I exhaled a breath of cigarette smoke and said, "Hi, Aunt Iris."

It wasn't the call I was hoping for, but my aunt's sweet, caring voice was the next best thing.

"How are ya, Aaron? I'm sorry it's been a few weeks since I called to check on ya, but I've been busy tending to Sarah."

God, I missed my aunt and my sweet niece so bad. "It's so great to hear your voice. Thank you for calling me. Your timing is always perfect."

We reminisced for a bit and had one of our typical 'check-in calls'. Talking to Iris was always a mixed bag of emotions as our conversations usually stirred up things from my past.

I vividly remember the day that Iris and Sarah picked me up from the correctional facility after my father was taken away and locked up for selling drugs. My stepmother had long since been dead from a fatal drug overdose. I wasn't even sure that the guy who was just incarcerated was my actual father. He certainly hadn't played the role of a father very well. The only 'family' I truly ever had was my aunt and my niece. I wondered if the emergency court appointment, which mandated my release into her custody, was the only reason that Iris was even involved in my life.

My aunt's first initiative was to force me to go back to school - a move that I abhorred due to the fact that I was constantly bullied by meatheads and jocks from the football team, while the girls in their high heels laughed at my scrawny body as they watched me get beaten to pulp. But I wasn't about to let that shit or my failing grades bring me down. Instead, I countered my physical ineptitude with excessive exercise and began working my ass off at the gym. This gave me the opportunity to work on my body for free and also work with some personal training clients so that I would have some extra dollars for tuition fees. In no time, the workouts paid off for me as I found myself pinning these bullies to the ground and burying them six feet under. My transformation was in full swing and I was no longer meek and weak.

I did lot of Pokemon card trading and made a few grand in my teenage years. I should have stuck to the card trading because I managed to lose all of my money in the stock market at the age of eighteen. Therefore, I decided to learn more about number crunching and the in's and out's and highs and lows of the stock market.

In college, I chose to major in finance, economics and psychology. I worked three jobs just to save for tuition toward my MBA. My first visit to Duke University was an outstanding experience. Almost 400 students from across the globe attended the open house. The school was awesome and the feeling of camaraderie was great. The professor walked in and blew us all away by remembering each candidate by name. I decided right then and there that this was the place that I wanted to be.

I spent all of my days and many sleepless nights preparing for the Graduate Management Admission Test, or GMAT as it is commonly known. I must say, somehow I always managed to outperform my own expectations. I passed the test with flying colors.

I kissed my niece on the cheek and strolled onto the campus at Duke with a newly acquired student loan of $50,000. I was riding high on my test results and my loan amount, until I discovered that at least 40 other students in my class had done just as well as me - some even better. I wanted to be the best, so it became clear that I was going to have to work very hard to do so in that highly competitive atmosphere.

I managed to excel to the point that in my last semester, I was able to strike a deal with a private brokerage in Manhattan. At that time, I thought it was in my best interest to move to Manhattan and work in a multi-billion-dollar company as the Principal Investment Banker.

I had a very productive first year there and the team was phenomenal; however, I found myself fantasizing about having a hot and sexy female boss. I would daydream about this sexy power-trip that I had concocted. I imagined that I would lay this bitch down on the conference room table after hours and fuck her in the boardroom when no one was there. Then, when that was no longer enough, I took my fantasies to another level and I imagined a quick fuck in the janitor's closet or a quickie from behind at the copier during office hours. But for now, I was stuck with an old man as my boss. At least the guy hired some hotties and had good taste in women. He also frequently invited me to some insanely rocking parties that he or his wealthy clients would throw from time to time.

The boss man was quite fond of younger women and somehow managed to keep up with them and please them beyond his wealth and age. I quickly figured out that I could learn a lot from this guy, hence I accepted an invitation from him to attend another party one evening. Certainly I could have done something on my own, but I had a hunch that I should go.

I descended in the elevator of the skyscraper that I worked in and met the boss man in the lobby. He had a limo waiting for us out front in the valet area.

We rolled up to this old industrial building, bailed out of the limo and strolled into the party, baller style. I noticed many of our past and existing clients were there and so was one of our competitors.

Then this tall, badass chick caught my attention as I passed her. She flashed me a smile and stopped and turned to look back at me.

"Would you like something?" she purred as she stopped and surveyed my empty hands (and I'm pretty sure the rest of my body too).

"Yes, of course," I answered as I cleared my throat and unbuttoned my collar button. I also shifted my leg in my pants to hide my burgeoning erection.

"Yeah, well what would you like?" she said as she bit her lower lip and cut her eyes down momentarily, as if to invite my eyes to do the same.

I obliged as I quickly glanced down at her name tag which read "Monica". I also mentally undressed her breasts at the same time.

"I will have you. And I think I would like to have you in a bittersweet, slow fashion." I took her phone and entered my number. "Call me," I said as I walked away with a glass of bourbon.

Minutes later, my phone dinged and I got a message from her, "Where should I head tonight after work?"

I smiled at her from across the room as I texted her my address to the penthouse.

While I was scanning the area for another potential prey, Monica kept running into me over and over, hinting that she couldn't wait any longer. She tapped me on my shoulder and leaned forward to whisper in my ear, “Would you like to have some more of that?”

I grabbed her by the elbow and dragged her across the dance floor. She showed no sign of resistance. As we reached the end of this big hall, I pushed her against the wall. She was trying to catch her breath - which I’m not sure if she lost from our fast strides across the dance floor or her adrenaline rush from being whisked away.

She was trying to make eye contact with me and read into my eyes. I couldn’t help myself and also couldn’t take my eyes off of her beautiful, porcelain-like body. My hands pressed against the wall and my arms formed a cage around her, trapping her and preventing her from escaping. I looked down at her gorgeous body. Hormones and adrenaline were coursing through my veins and my dick was swelling up in my pants. I wanted her so fucking bad that I couldn’t contain my emotions. I had to release the physical angst, so I punched the wall with the heel of my hand only inches away from her face. I couldn’t hurt a delicate flower, so the wall had to take the brunt of my alcohol and hormone-induced rage. I looked down, trying to look away from her and not seal her fate with me that night.

She was shocked and taken aback as my hand whizzed past her face and connected with the wall. She quivered, but relaxed as she took a second to hold my face with her soft, but cold hands. She looked into my eyes and pressed her lips against mine. I grabbed her wrists and moved her arms forcefully above her head, pressing my body against hers. I controlled her quivers by frantically kissing her, but ultimately, that wasn’t enough.

I lifted up her skirt up and shoved my hands into her panties. Just as I expected - hardwood floors, no rug. Her pussy was smooth and clean. That's what I like - smooth as silk down there. I slid my hand across her thigh and into her 'v' between her leg and her hip. As I slid further down, things got wet and sticky with no warning. I squeezed her inner thigh to open her pussy lips ever so slightly and then I pierced her vagina with my finger. She flexed her calves to gain some height as she leaned her body against mine. She moaned in my ear as she nibbled my neck and dug her fingernails into my shoulders.

I pushed her back down flat onto her feet and forced my finger deeper inside of her box. She moaned loudly as she arched her back. Her body began trembling and she quickly lost her breath. She unbuckled my belt and I simultaneously slid a second finger inside of her.

Just as she was about to slide her hands inside of my Jockeys, I pulled her into the family room adjacent to us. Our newfound privacy immediately changed her demeanor as she stripped down and came on strong. She took my dick into her mouth and tongued the precum off of its tip. I held her hair back as she enjoyed the taste. Then, she proceeded to jam my cum gun into each and every one of her orifices.

She turned her head to look back at me as she bent over further and spread her ass cheeks wider. Who could resist that? I pounded that ass until she begged me to stop from the intense ecstasy and pain. I didn't last much longer anyway and shot my load in her ass. We both got dressed quickly and left the family room and strolled back into the party in separate directions with smiles on our faces and my souvenir in her ass.

The next day, I heard the bell ring and I saw her on the security camera. She was all dolled up and ready to get fucked again. Round two, round three, as well as the next fifty proved to be even more erotic than our first fuck at the party. We fucked for the next few months in every square inch of my penthouse and we christened every piece of furniture that I owned. She effectively marked her territory and then laid the ultimate claim and moved right on in with me. She justified the move, citing that it would make her proximity to the modeling agency closer and her drive to work easier - at least until she landed a big television acting gig.

One night, we were just hanging out and the devil got into me. I could sense that work stress was mounting, as a result of which, we were losing our connection and lust. She was anxiously checking her phone frequently to see if her modeling gig or her acting audition had come through. There was nothing I could do about that, but I knew what I could do, so I took matters into my own hands.

"Hey babe, I want you to be my bitch tonight. I'm gonna fuck the worry right out of you," I said as I spun her around on the bar stool and removed the cell phone from her hand.

I grabbed her smooth, sexy legs and spread them wide. I slid my finger between her short shorts and her inner thighs until I reached her panties. With a slight bend of my finger, I infiltrated her panties and began to tickle her clit. She moaned and shuddered with delight, confirming my hunch that she just needed some sexual healing to help her forget her work related stress. We fucked all night and passed out in each other's arms.

Over the next month, I learned that sex will only take you so far in a relationship. Our sex life had been fantastic, but our friendship was waning. More often than not, she was gone for long hours and sometimes all night as well. When she was home, she would sit on her computer or her phone, texting incessantly. Whatever she was doing, caused her mixed emotions as she vacillated between smiling and stressing. There were times she would smile while looking at her phone or computer screen, but these days, I could see her eyebrows raised and her brow furrowed. She would snap if I touched her in anyway. I concluded that it was time to have a very serious talk.

I started off positive and conversational rather than confrontational. "Babe, how are you doing today? How's work going? Anything new come up?"

With a lump in her throat and her phone clutched in her trembling hands, she said, "I think we need to talk."

I recognized this behavior. Unfortunately, it was the same behavior I had witnessed in the past when my father was strung out on drugs. I knew she was in some sort of trouble, but I couldn't anticipate the extent of it.

I gently started my inquisition. "Babe, are you on drugs or something? Have you been smoking or snorting something or popping pills? What's wrong, girl?"

Based on my past interactions with addicts, I wasn't expecting to her to continue this conversation the way that I wanted, but I was wrong!

She proceeded to open up and come clean about how she had joined an online chatting/dating community before meeting me and that she had become involved with a guy. She claimed it wasn't serious, so she didn't bother to tell me. From what I understood, she shared her phone number and some pictures with him... and then they had some sexting episodes... which was followed by sex on web cam. This guy she was involved with had the cam recorded and he supplied the videos to a porn website. She started crying as she continued to reveal her secret. I was pissed, but I tried to be a compassionate listener. Now she said that he is stalking her, and recently made her get in his bed. I grew angrier by the second, but I contained my angst and continued to listen. And then came the part I suspected - he had got her hooked on drugs and then introduced her to a bunch of his other friends. Although she became overwhelmed by emotion and tears and curtailed her story, I could only assume that she had sex with these 'other friends' as well. I was enraged, but I consoled her and resolved to myself to get to the bottom of the situation.

I decided to confront this guy who was responsible for the corruption of my girl, so I swiped her phone and laptop and scanned all of her chat and browsing history. Luckily, I had made some connections with a gang of hackers while I was working my way up the ranks in the financial world. Hackers were particularly useful to find out information on people - as well as business and trade secrets from companies and their executives. From call girls to hackers and spies, I had done whatever it took to get ahead in life.

I called a rookie from the hacker gang I had previously used because I knew that he would work cheap and not fear the outcome of revealing personal information acquired by unlawful means. All he asked me to do was to provide access to her laptop so that he could remotely control it. The only thing that I had to do was to keep the battery charged and the laptop running.

This guy proved to be a master of his trade because in just a couple of hours, he came up with the guy's exact street address. Adrenaline coursed through my veins as I grabbed my jacket, jumped in the car and programmed my navigation to take me to his location.

The location turned out to be a luxury apartment building in downtown Manhattan. I managed to breeze by the doorman and security guard who nodded at me and waved me by. Apparently, they were more interested in watching a football game than paying attention to the security of the building. I took note of the plethora of security cameras in the lobby and the hallway to the elevators.

As I pressed the button for the 18th floor and the elevator started to ascend, I debated why the doorman had let me in at 3 AM without checking my ID or at least questioning me. I got paranoid and wondered whether he was somehow aware that I was Monica's boyfriend. I felt my fist squeeze tighter and my jaw clench harder. I was ready to throw down if necessary.

I exited the elevator and took a left in the hallway and made my way towards the end of the hall where unit #C6 was located. I took a deep breath and composed myself. Knock. Knock.

I waited patiently and then knocked again, this time louder. No response. Seconds felt like hours as I was running out of patience and wanted to kick the door open.

Just as I was about to knock again, a guy swung the door open. He stood there in his boxers as he surveyed me from head to toe. And then, he chuckled. I wanted to punch him in his fucking nose right then and there, but before I could, he addressed me and shocked me.

"Hello, Aaron," he said with a cocky smirk and a nod as he continued to size me up.

I had never seen this guy in my entire life; so needless to say, I was fucking shocked that he knew my name. I responded accordingly, "You know who I am?"

"Yes, I know everything about you," he said in an arrogant tone as he turned his back on me and walked back into his apartment, leaving the door open as if to invite me to follow. "I know what you do, where you work, how much money you have, and which girl you're banging," he said, as he leaned over the kitchen counter to snort a line of coke.

I scanned the apartment for a second as he got high. The decor was basic and the furnishings were Spartan; however, there was a king sized mattress in the middle of the living room - on which there was a black sheet with a stoned naked girl laying on it. There wasn't much food visible in the kitchen, but there was a bunch of laptops sitting on the kitchen counter along with a stash of smokes and some pills in a bowl, with a gun sitting atop a stack of files.

I felt like this guy had actually been expecting me somehow. I sensed that there was something deep and incomprehensible to all of this - a trap maybe? I realized I couldn't pull myself out of the trap, unless I found out what I was into. My anger translated into intimidation.

"What do you want from me?" I asked sternly.

He laughed as he squeezed his nose and shook his head as if to fully absorb and appreciate the cocaine that he had just snorted.

"Why do you think I want something from you and not your girlfriend?" he asked as he slowly moved across the room and picked up a laptop. He plopped down on the corner of the mattress next to the stoned, naked chick.

His arrogance was overwhelming to me. I considered picking up his gun and unloading the clip into his filthy body, but I knew that if I killed him, I would never get resolution or answers, so I chose to answer his question instead. "For the fact that you have not kicked me out, nor have you killed me yet."

He smiled with a pompous arrogance as he cut his eyes up to me from the laptop screen. "You're correct. I'm glad we're on the same page - you and me." His eyes returned to the laptop, but he continued his questions. “So tell me Aaron, did your girlfriend tell you that she is a porn pimp? And that she has been running this porn website with me for the last few years?” he said as he spun the laptop around to reveal the page he was speaking of.

I squinted to see the screen from a distance, but it was clear to me that it was porn and that the images were hers. I was fucking furious, but I contained my emotions and let him continue.

“Before she even met you, we were together and she made lots of money for me,” he said as he confidently grinned and nodded his head in approval of his own statement. “After getting in bed with you, she has become somewhat incompetent. Let’s just say that business has suffered tremendously because of you, Aaron.” His eyes cut back to me and his shit-eating grin turned into a stern and serious lock-jawed look. “So you need to make up for all the money that I lost,” he said as he glared at me.

In my head, I quickly and repeatedly envisioned how I could kill this asshole with his own gun that was lying next to me. As enraged as I was at the moment and as tempting as it was to kill this fucker, I took a moment to consider the consequences of murder. After all, I realized now that ‘my’ girl was never truly mine. Plus, I wanted to find out everything this guy knew about me and whether he had any accomplices. He talked about a lot of money, so I wanted to find out just how much and how I could potentially get my share too.

He calmed his demeanor and invited me to sit on the edge of the bed with him and the naked girl. I got a closer look at her and I realized that she was fucking HOT, but I wasn't sure if she was even alive. I stared at her bare breasts for a moment until I saw her chest rise and fall, indicating that she was breathing. I sighed with relief and then immediately wondered whether he was inviting me to have a threesome. Instead, he proceeded to show me a bunch of websites that he had open on the laptop.

He handed the laptop over to me and left me sitting on the edge of the mattress, inches away from the passed-out hottie who reeked of marijuana and sex. He walked towards the kitchen and looked at his phone. He grabbed a smoke from his pack of Marlboros and then gestured to me as he tossed the pack across the room to me. I really needed a smoke at the time to get me through this wilderness.

I returned my attention to the website as I toked on the cigarette. The first website was a chatting/dating website which had text, voice and cam features available for both private and group interaction.

"So how do I login to this website?" I asked.

"You can use my email ID to login for now." He said as he spelled out his email address for me.

Then he walked me through the ins and outs of the app.

I was surprised how quickly I learned how the group and private channels functioned. I also noticed on one of his open websites that he had some money invested and a total of over $10k in credit points.

I moved to another website that he showed me. This one was a semi-porn site with webcams of guys and girls helping themselves to each other. The website had a tracker that captured the exact IP address and location of a user, thus allowing him to trace the location of all the users. He also introduced me to the concept of 'bots', which he used to control the chat website. This guy was no charmer, rather a very rough and crude sack of shit.

I quickly realized that this guy was using my girlfriend to lure rich men into his realm so that he could profitize from the website. Then he would further entangle other women into his web by supplying them with whatever they needed - sex, drugs, immigration status… I'm sure the list goes on. I couldn't even fathom how many women he had used and profited from.

Even though I was initially infuriated and repulsed by what this guy was doing to women, I found myself enthralled with the business model and his success. The next thing I knew, I went from looking at porn sites to setting up one of my own with this guy's help. I found myself debating what nickname and profile pic to use.

I wanted to trump this guy's fake ego and establish the fact that I intended to be the boss, so I chose to use the online ID and nickname 'Alpha'. This was to be my online moniker as well as describe my new persona. I wanted to send a clear message that I was the Alpha male!

He chuckled as I typed in my new nickname while he observed me and my progress. He suggested a profile picture for me to use from the gallery on my phone and also recommended that I shade it to grayscale when I upload it. I was a little concerned and nervous about using my actual picture, so I questioned his recommendation.

"Why should I use my own image on my profile?"

"You are a good looking man and well spoken. You don't need to exert a lot of extra effort like I have to. Yet I only get desperate, married women."

"So I have to use my looks, my financial status and my education to seduce a single woman?"

"Not just one single woman, but rich single WOMEN!"

"How does that help you?"

"Just get them on cam and I will take care of the rest. You don't have to worry about a thing," he said as he nodded his head and flashed his devilish smile again.

It sounded easy enough. In fact, a little too easy and sleazy. I questioned my safety.

"Can you guarantee my safety and that my personal information will be kept secure?"

"Trust me, you don't have to worry about a thing. We will not use your actual image without morphing it a little bit to blur the details of your face."

“What about my voice?”

“We have a software for that as well. We will not put our assets in jeopardy.”

“Assets? As in more than one? I don't work like that. I want to be the only asset.”

“We will wait and see how things shape up in the future, but for now, I can’t make any promises.”

I put all emotion and intrigue aside for a moment and reflected on the whole situation.

“What if I refuse to do any of this and simply walk away?”

He smirked and retorted, “No problem, I will just make a phone call to the local news agency and let them know that you have a pimp in your house that runs an illegal porn website. It won’t be hard for the cops to associate your IP address to the website. I am sure you don’t want to follow in your father’s footsteps and end up in jail.”

I put the laptop down, got up and walked out through the sliding glass doors onto the balcony. The cold winter air was refreshing. ‘What the fuck have I gotten myself into?’ I thought. I considered just sending Monica back to him after I dumped the bitch. Yet somehow, I was still compelled to move forward with his twisted game. Maybe it was my fear of losing my job, if this guy blackmailed me and blew the whistle on Monica - or maybe it was a hidden desire to participate in this filthy scheme. I took a deep breath of fresh air and re-entered the apartment.

"Alright, I will help you recoup the $250k that you claim you lost because of my relationship with Monica. But we are done after that," I said with confidence, knowing full well that there was no guarantee that he wouldn't blackmail me anyway. I knew that I had to concoct an exit strategy if I wanted a way out. Maybe I would become incompetent so that he is compelled to fire me - or maybe in time, I could find someone to replace me. I knew either ploy would take some time to enact.

I figured that getting him the $250k would take about a year based on his projections. I thought I could expedite the process by baiting a big fish worth millions, who wouldn't mind throwing a few $100k at this guy and his online ventures. In the meantime, I would start luring girls into his cave - and then what he does with them is none of my business.

I reluctantly shook his hand and agreed to move forward. Then I realized, I didn't even know his name. So I asked, "So what is your name anyway?"

He laughed a lot. "Online I am Cobra, but you can call me Sam."

I sent dozens of girls his way and made him shitloads of money over the next few months, but now I was over it and ready to retire. I started slacking and not doing much for him, which he quickly realized. I openly expressed my desire to get out of the deal. Much to my surprise and delight, he agreed to let me go - on one condition. He wanted me to bait one more girl, who owned a billion-dollar art gallery.

My phone rang and I answered it to hear Cobra's voice. He ecstatically asked, "Can we meet up?"

"Is it urgent?" I asked.

"Yes, I have the last one for you. Get me in with this one and you are free to go. I have a file on her. Can you come tomorrow and pick it up?"

"Fine, I will stop by after work today."

I could taste my freedom as I drove to his downtown luxury apartment for the last time. When I arrived, I found the door to his penthouse cracked so I walked in and made my way into his kitchen, for what I hoped would be the last time. There lay the file on the kitchen counter. As I picked up the file, Sam emerged from the living room to greet me. We wasted no time in starting to go over the financial records, locations of the art galleries, image of the target and her friends, etc… I perused the entire file for a moment and then glanced up and made direct and focused eye contact with Sam, before I asked, "So after this one, I'm done?"

He patted me on the shoulder and then walked me to the door. "Call me when you've got something on her. She ain't gonna be easy!"

I smiled all the way home as I kept glancing over at the file lying in my passenger seat. 'She is my way out of this,' I thought. When I got home, I dove right into reviewing the file and researching as much information as I could find on her. I was disappointed to discover that she was not on iVoice, as that was going to be my best way to get to her and the only way to properly deliver her to Sam. I decided to call her, pretending to be a sales rep and introduce her to a free chatting application.

I used the voice changer app that Sam had demonstrated for me. I figured it would make me sound more like a telemarketer. After a couple of trial runs on the phone with Sam, he gave me the green light to go ahead and call her. The anticipation was killing me as the phone rang and rang with no answer.

It was a very anticlimactic disappointment. I considered leaving a voicemail, but then decided that telemarketers don't leave voicemails, so I didn't. I could hear her voice on the automated message preceding the beep. When the beep tone hit my eardrum, I followed my instinct and just hung up.

I called her for the next few days in a row, before I realized that I needed to change my strategy. I cleverly concocted a plan and then texted her an 'introductory offer', with a link to download a free version of the iVoice app. On the back end, I was tracing the link to see if she opened it. Sure enough, the next day - BINGO, she opened it and downloaded it. Sam then traced her IP address and found her exact location. Everything was coming together nicely so far!

The very next day, I found her on Channel 1 and I introduced myself. It was a fun chat. She was kinda all over the place and seemed to be a very happy-go-lucky girl. We talked about her family, friends, hobbies, relationships and a recent breakup. She was an open book and quite wild with her imagination. I did try to get her on cam, but she outright refused; however, she did hit me up on voice chat again later!

"Hey, what's up, Dor?" I asked as I tried to contain my excitement over the fact that she had reached out to me.

"Nothing much. I am tired of being bored and I need to get laid," she said in a super seductive tone.

I took a drag off of my smoke, smiled and answered, "God, you are crazy woman!"

"How crazy am I?" she said inquisitively. "Am I crazy enough to turn you on?"

I played it cool and coy, "It takes a lot to turn me on, babe."

"I can't wait to meet you. Why don't you meet me at this party in Jersey this Saturday night?" she cooed.

"Where is this party?" I asked as I became extremely excited.

"Not far. I am texting you the address now."

"Will you be alone? Or will you have a friend tagging along?" I asked, in hope of getting the answer I desired.

"I will be alone," she said, much to my chagrin.

I thought quick and suggested, "Why not plan for a threesome? I can totally handle cumming more than once!"

"You're kidding me, right?" she answered, but I couldn't tell if she was disgusted or interested.

I didn't know how to respond. I didn't want to say anything to blow the rapport I was building, so I simply said, "Nope. I'm dead serious!"

"Well then, I've got a challenge for you. I've got this friend - she's hot and nice, but she's a total prude. I'm not sure if she could get wet if she fell into a swimming pool. I bet you couldn't turn her on."

"Challenge accepted, bring her!" I eagerly replied. "By the way, how will I find you, since you won't let me see you on cam or even send me a pic?"

She giggled, "Just wear some red Jockey underwear, hottie - I'll handle the rest!"

I added buying some red Jockeys to my to-do list before asking my final, all-important question, "So who is this friend of yours? Tell me about her."

"Well, she seems to never do or say anything wrong. In fact, I'm not sure if I've ever heard her curse. She was born a millionaire and she now owns a bunch of art galleries that she inherited when her father died. Poor girl, she had already lost her mother at a very young age. I think she needs to cut loose and have some fun and take a break from her mundane life."

"Well, I'll see what I can do to bring her out of her shell," I stated with confidence before I said goodbye and hung up the call.

The scheme was coming together nicely. I was ecstatic to call Sam the next day and inform him that I had a better deal for him.

"Hey Sam, who's the man?" I said with an air of cockiness.

"So, whatcha got?" he asked with a certain degree of coolness.

"Dude, we have two girls now at the same party. Either you can take one, or I'm going to have myself a threesome! Send me a pic of yourself so I can pass it on to the girls to seal the deal."

"Good work, Aaron. I'll send you an enhanced image. Get it done and pick me up tomorrow."

I received his pic and then shot it over to Dor and confirmed that I would be at the party with him.

The next day, I picked up Sam in my car and we drove over to the party. We were both stunned by the size and splendor of the New Jersey villa where the party was being held. It was definitely my kind of place - filled with booze and a lot of hot chicks! I was stoked to discover that there was a pool there overlooking a creek and a beautifully landscaped backyard. I envisioned getting naked with a hot girl in the pool and then banging her under the dark, starlit sky - but first, we made our way through the house and mingled with some other guests. I had a few drinks, popped a couple of pills and smoked a joint.

We scanned the party for Dor and her friend, but I had no idea what either of them looked like, so I kept a close eye on the front door and driveway, hoping to see two single girls arriving. Sure enough, a limo pulled up and out popped two gorgeous ladies. One appeared to be very confident and sassy while the other seemed timid as it took her a moment to get out of the limo. Both were beautiful, but the latter looked stunning in her little black dress, while the former lit up a cigarette. They both lingered outside of the limo for a moment. I assumed they were chatting for a moment before entering the party, but I was shocked to see the girl that I assumed was Dor, grab her friend, spin her around and proceed to lay a 'more than friendly' kiss on her! I prayed those two to be our targets! They finally entered the party and I signaled Sam from across the room, but he was tied up at the bar getting a drink. The two girls quickly separated and I followed the friend in the black dress from a distance. She was parading through the party, but nothing seemed to interest her.

I followed her out to the pool area and I imagined her and myself jumping in naked, but instead, she walked past the pool and into the landscaping down by the creek. I watched as she sat on a rock wall and stared off into the distance as if she was in deep reflection. I wanted to approach her, but it seemed like she was content being alone for the moment, plus I didn't want to seem too eager or stalker-like. And then the pills I had popped started to kick in along with the weed I had smoked. I decided to just sit down by the pool and wait for her to walk back up.

As I sat there waiting and anticipating her next course of action, a bunch of drunk girls came over to the pool. Several guys followed them and hovered close by the pool as the girls proceeded to shed their dresses and lingerie, and jump right in for a skinny-dip! It didn't take long for the guys to follow suit. Clothes went flying and water was splashing everywhere. I took a quick count to inventory the bodies in the pool. It seemed that there was one less guy than girls in the pool and coincidentally, the one solo girl winked at me. So I did the proper thing and stripped down and dove in to join them! My naked pool fantasy was in full swing as I began to splash and wrestle around with my new friend. I kept a careful watch out of the corner of my eye for the girl in the black dress to emerge from the back yard; however, for the moment, the bird in hand was better than the one down in the bushes!

It must have been a while because I was in the midst of full-on frolicking when I finally saw her stroll across the pool deck in her short black dress. She turned to glance at the commotion in the pool. We had a very brief eye contact, which made me smile. I couldn't resist her naive eyes as she smiled back at me, but then she looked right through me and promptly walked away.

The next thing I knew, I was abandoning my 'sure thing' in the pool and drying off with someone else's shirt. I put my pants on and re-entered the party, still dripping wet from my hasty and inadequate drying-off. I scanned the party and saw Dor talking to someone, but I didn't see the girl in the black dress. I kept searching frantically and then I saw her standing out front at the valet, just as her limo pulled up. I made a dash for the front door, but missed her by seconds as she hopped in the back of the limo and took off.

Against my better judgment, I forgot my deal with Sam as well as the fact that I was inebriated, as I hailed the valet to get my car. I patiently waited as he pulled my car up and then I jumped in and attempted to catch up to the limo. I finally caught up, but stayed back a ways and followed from a distance as the limo drove through the city. At one point, she rolled the back window down and hung her head slightly out of the car, just enough for her hair to blow in the wind. I was smitten with her.

I followed the limo until it pulled up to what I assumed was her house. I watched her exit the limo and saunter up to her place. I just sat there in my car staring up at her window like a schoolboy in love for the very first time. I couldn't stop smiling.

Chapter Four

Crisis

After a long day at work, I said goodbye to Mrs. Martha and headed home. I hoped to get relief from the stress of a day at the gallery by checking my phone as soon as I got home. Hoping for a call or text from Phantom, I was disappointed. It had been a day since our last conversation and our 3rd e-date. I knew the ball was in my court to decide whether I would move forward and continue my online relationship with him, but a call or text would have been nice. My curiosity led me to check channel 1 to see if he was on the group chat.

I didn't find Phantom, but I did meet a new guy who was on Channel 1 asking for someone to help him with the app's privacy settings. It was easy for me to feel sorry for him because his situation reminded me of how I had felt on my first day using the app. I couldn't understand why no one else on the channel had jumped in to help him and answer any of his numerous questions and pleas for help. Ultimately, I decided to end 'Newguyintown's' agony and help him since I couldn't help but feel sorry for him. So I shot him a message and asked how I could help - and then he insisted on a private message.

This guy was either not very bright or he was playing some sort of game. He complained about getting porn spam messages. I tried to calm him down and walked him through the steps to set up his privacy settings so that he would only get messages from people who he had accepted on his instant messenger list. We went step by step together, but he claimed that it wasn't working and that he was still getting spam. I'm no tech genius by any means, but I just couldn't figure out how it didn't work. I also couldn't fathom how he was getting so much spam so frequently. Then his true motives were exposed.

He jumped from a tech support conversation to asking me, "So do you have a boyfriend?"

"No, I don't," I responded, slightly annoyed.

"How is that possible? You have such a beautiful voice. Not even an e-boyfriend?"

"Thank you, but nope. I'm single and not ready to mingle."

"Okay, can you please call me so that I can work through this damn privacy setting situation?"

"No. I'm not trying to give out my digits to strangers on this app."

"I don't want your number. You call me," he reasoned.

"Well, if I call you, then you'll have my number on your caller ID."

"You can always block your number. Just go into your phone settings and block your number or call your service provider and they can tell you how to put the block on."

"Nah, I'll pass. You'll figure it out on your own," I said as I politely excused myself from calling him and ended the message exchange.

The very next day, I saw Newguyintown repeating the same thing on Channel 1. He really had no clue what he was doing on here. I guessed he must be very young, maybe in college or something. I ignored him this time.

I thought it was very strange that he knew enough about technology to block a phone number, but couldn't figure out how to work the privacy settings on iVoice. Nonetheless, he was persistent and I finally started to feel pity for the guy, so I blocked my number and gave him a call. He put his headset on so that his hands were free and followed my instructions as I verbally walked him through the privacy settings on the app. We were able to determine that he did not have a virus and got his settings right. This time it seemed to work nicely. He thanked me and after a brief chat about technology, we hung up.

Just when I thought my interaction with him was done, he pinged me again an hour later.

"Hey Angel, thanks for your help with the app. It's working great now. No more porn spam! Let's talk over the phone again. Give me your digits."

Further annoyed that he asked for my number yet again, I rejected his invite to chat with a white lie, "No, I am on another call."

He laughed and asked, "Really? So who are you talking to?"

"I'm talking to my only friend on this app."

"Does your friend have a name?" he asked with a curious laugh.

"If you must know, he goes by Phantom."

He then proceeded to laugh to himself in almost a sinister tone.

"Why do you laugh like that?" I asked. "You sound like a ghost, laughing to yourself like that. What is so funny?"

"I laugh because I know your friend Phantom very well. He's quite popular with the gals online."

"That's weird, he said he was new here on this app."

"He calls me his best friend and he's like a brother to me. I actually know him very well - I taught him how to rule the chat world," he said as he paced back and forth, trying to postpone nature's call.

"That's interesting!" I said, wanting to know more, but 'Newguyintown' abruptly said he needed to go to the restroom. I asked him if he wanted me to hold, but he said it might be a while, so he disconnected from the chat and went offline.

This really bothered me to think that Phantom lied to me about being new on the app. Plus, this guy claims that he's basically an online player. I couldn't get over the shock. I felt a pit develop in my stomach. I dwelled on it for hours until 'Newguyintown' popped back online and messaged me again.

"Let's do a voice chat," he suggested.

"Wow, that was the longest bathroom break in history!"

I hesitantly agreed to the voice chat, but for some reason through the course of our conversation, I felt compelled to open up and introduce myself. I spoke from the heart, truthfully as I told him how I lived in the sunshine state and about the passing of my mom and dad. He listened, but didn't really take interest in my location or my family (or lack thereof).

"Do you have a boyfriend?" he asked, interrupting me.

"No. I am single, but not ready to mingle," I said, slightly aggravated that he had interrupted the story about my parents - and asked yet another question that I had already answered.

"Well then, do you have a girlfriend?" he asked jokingly. We both laughed at his insinuation that I was a lesbian.

"I am very much straight," I proudly announced to quell that direction of the conversation.

“Show me your picture,” he pretty much demanded.

“Sorry, no picture or cam,” I fired back immediately.

"Ok, well, describe yourself then. How tall are you?”

After thinking for a few seconds, I decided to mess with him. "I am four feet tall."

He was silent for a second and then said in shock, “Oh.” That was all he said in response.

I couldn’t control my laughter, but I suppressed it and kept it to myself.

"Um, so how much do you weigh?"

"Oh, I am not that heavy. Merely 180 lbs,” I said as I snickered to myself.

He let out an audible laugh that I think he choked on a little bit. "Good, good. A lot to enjoy!”

I didn’t understand his sarcasm, and I’m not sure if he caught my humor or if he thought I was serious.

Then he caught [me] off guard. "I have an advice for you… don’t talk to Phantom anymore. You might regret it later.”

"That’s funny, he says the same about everyone else on here," I said in Phantom’s defense.

"Well, if you don't believe me, you can talk to Monica. She is trustworthy."

"Alright, I'll take that into consideration then," I said as I rolled my eyes and prepared myself to end the conversation.

"Fine, I'll talk to you later then. I am going to the gym," he said with sarcasm. "By the way, this New Year's party is gonna be in Vegas, baby. For my cousin's bachelor party."

I had no idea why he was telling me this. "That's great!" I said as I filed my nails.

"Do you go to the gym?"

"No, I don't. I don't need to."

"Whatever. You just said that you were 4-foot-tall and weighed 180 pounds. Are you so fat that you can't even walk on a treadmill?"

"Who said I am fat? I am slim."

"You did. You said that. Are you messing with me? Like how slim are you?"

"I'm like a size 2."

"Ah! You should put some fat on your bones in all the right places. You know what I mean?"

I didn't reply to his crass comment.

"Now I need visual evidence. Prove it. I need to know for sure that you are size 2. Here are your options: A) Switch on your webcam - or B) I am flying to Tampa this Wednesday and you can come pick me up from the airport."

"Nope. I am not doing any of it. And I have nothing to prove to you or anyone else here. I know what I am and I am happy with it. Size 2 or size 20. So be it," I affirmed. There's no way this jerk was going to body shame me. Grrrrrrrrr!!!

In order to preserve my sanity and stay off of the chat channels, I tried my best not to think of any of the users - particularly Phantom. I put on my gym clothes and went out for a run and then practiced my kickboxing moves afterward to release some additional stress that the run didn't relieve. Then I got back home and walked the dog before cleaning every inch of my kitchen. I immersed myself in these chores for some time and avoided being online immediately after my conversation with Newguyintown.

Later, I jumped back on chat and exchanged a few words with Monica. She seemed nice to me, but you can never be sure; after all, it's all behind the anonymity of a computer screen. Weird thoughts popped into my head. What if Phantom and Newguyintown were the same person. Nah. Ridiculous. Then I thought some more. What if Monica is Phantom's girlfriend or cousin or something - even a friend with benefits. My mind ran wild with these absurd ideas. The world-wide web is a big place, I told myself. Plus, Monica is from California and Phantom is from Long Island. There's no way that they could have a long-distance relationship from that far!

To keep my head from spinning over all of the online drama, I indulged myself in work and spent as much time with Mrs. Martha as possible. She suggested that I revisit some of my hobbies like playing the keyboard or even booking another skydiving session. I attempted to exhaust myself so that I would simply fall asleep at night, but exercise and house cleaning wasn't enough to fulfil me completely, so I resolved to take her advice, but I soon caved in again and defaulted back to the chat world.

The same night I decided to login to the main chat room, determined to avoid both Newguyintown and Phantom until I could figure out who was who and what was what.

I noticed a guy with the nickname 'Notorious' dominating the conversation on the channel. He was carrying on about hacking someone's IP address and releasing all of their personal details. He flashed a serial number, an IP address, and then proceeded to say, "...and her name starts with T … A......N....... Now let me find her location. Oh, she is from the sunshine state. And her phone number is… 813…" My heart was racing and it even skipped a few beats. I couldn't believe what just happened.

Monica intervened, "Oh, come on Cobra, don't do it to that poor gal. She might not like that."

Then they both simultaneously let out a sinister laugh.

Soon after, Notorious sent me a private voice message. His voice seemed very familiar, but it wasn't Phantom, for sure. Then I realized, oh my Lord - it's Newguyintown. Both nicknames were the same person. Newguyintown is Notorious - and Monica just said 'Cobra don't do this to her', indicating that it was also Cobra. How appropriate - a triad of evil jerks!

Notorious messaged me again. "Hey Angel, this is Newguyintown."

"Yeah, I just figured that out. I don't wanna talk to you."

"Look, let me just explain, it was a joke, nothing personal."

"Yes, it was very personal. All of my personal info, in fact." With that infuriated rebuttal, I disconnected and logged off.

I didn't reply to him anymore, nor did he pursue me. He is a scam artist, broadcasting my personal information out on the world-wide web. It's amazing how mean some people can be. Surely this app is not a place for me, but I'll be damned if I'm going to let these jokers get away with this. I feared that I was going to become a vengeful person. Once I entangle myself with revenge, nothing can stop me. I take pleasure in being a slow poison to my enemies - and preventing them from doing this again comforts me even more.

This was not easy as my mind was already corrupted. I started scheming my big revenge. The problem was, I had no idea who he was and how he operated, but surely he was friends with Phantom and Monica.

I bravely ventured back onto the app, with the purpose of playing detective, but strangely each night, new error messages flashed when I tried to login. The next night, I got endless friend requests from clone IDs which crashed the app. After an hour, I tried again, but this time channel 1 was full of bots. No one was speaking or texting - it was all just dead air and a bunch of bots.

Then I got a lucky message from a guy named Venom.

“Hi Iron Angel, come to channel 12.”

I joined the channel with ease and there I met Rebel Queen, Rex and of course, my invitee Venom.

Venom introduced me and welcomed me to the channel.

“Hey guys, thanks for the invite. So what's the hot topic? And what’s going on with Channel 1?” I asked.

Rebel Queen responded, “Yes, I know. There are so many clones and bot IDs. I think Cobra is back.”

I wondered what she meant and what she knew, so I asked, “Who is Cobra and how do you know him?”

“Who doesn’t know him? He is evil - stay away from him!”

"Yeah, that's what everyone else says also. But I'm not worried, he can't do anything. There are laws in place that cover this kind of thing."

"Don't fall for his crap. We must warn other people too," she insisted. "By the way, do you know Monica?"

"Yes I do," I replied without hesitation.

Rex chimed in, "She is a real bitch."

Rebel Queen added, "She pretended to be in love with a guy for three months and took expensive gifts from him and then just vanished."

Rex affirmed, "She got back on another chat with a different boyfriend. Those three really messed up the chat world for a few months."

I squinted my eyes and furrowed my brow. "Three? Who was the guy and who was the boyfriend?"

I wondered if I was totally being taken for a ride. What if everyone was lying to me? I was sick to my stomach and quickly losing my temper.

Rebel Queen answered immediately, "Phantom aka Alpha is her boy toy and her boyfriend is Cobra." Then she went on to elaborate more on how these three characters were troublemakers.

I gulped, "Gosh."

To which she responded, "Well, I have a story of my own. I was dating this guy online for two years and I totally fell in love with him. I finally put my fears aside and asked him for an actual date, but he shot me down and refused. He gave me some lame excuse that he had an important office audition the very same week. But I was tangled up in his emotional web, so I asked him out again - and again he refused due to some 'personal family issue.' I kept on falling for his bait for another year, opening up and giving him my personal info, like my name, cell phone number and my location. Then one day, he just decided that he didn't like me anymore and cut me off online. He said that I was being too possessive."

I listened intently as Rex then opened up and shared a story about his own love triangle in which he lost the love of his life to another chatmate. Then I decided to share my own story of how I learned of Cobra's multiple accounts and how he exposed my personal info on a group chat at Channel 1.

Venom broke his silence, "Cobra is a bloody criminal!"

"He is from Canada, right?" Rex asked.

Venom answered, "No, he is from New York City. He owns a malicious website where he posts objectionable content."

"I think he's been there for like 10 years," Rex added.

I tried to follow the conversation, but got lost for a second, "What are you guys talking about?"

Venom then pinged me on a private message, “Hey Angel, I don’t want to reveal anything or even talk about Cobra on the main chat. Can we chat over the mic for a minute?”

I agreed and he continued, “How could a smart girl like you fall for a con man like him?" His tone had a slight air of sarcasm - apparently he was making fun of me.

"Well I am way too straightforward to understand that some twisted people cause trouble to others for no reason,” I confidently shot back.

Venom went on to tell me that Cobra had been on the app for a decade. He was a college dropout who amused himself by flirting with girls. To earn money, he forged documents and later created a pornography site which targeted chat room girls on webcam. He also bought and sold a couple of businesses for profit. Now, he just enjoys breaking innocent hearts.

I was curious how Venom knew so much about him, so I asked and he replied, “He is so pompous that he used to brag about his deeds on the main chat.”

"Wow, I really can’t believe that I had been talking to such an infamous and scandalous man all this time,” I said in shock.

“Please tell me that you didn’t show him your cam or picture,” Venom said, fumbling for the right words to ask me without crossing any lines or offending me.

"No, I didn’t," I answered confidently.

"Did you call him?" he asked inquisitively.

"Yes, I did call him."

Venom laughed, “So he has your digits now."

“How is that possible? I blocked my number.”

"If only it was that easy. There are some apps available that reveal blocked numbers. You can buy the subscriptions to them online.”

"I’m puzzled, what’s the point? Just so he can call me? It’s been a few days and he hasn’t called me.”

Venom huffed, "Cobra is a big-time playa - either you’re a small bait for him or he is just waiting to bring action to his next plan."

I decided to shift the conversation to satisfy my other curiosity. "Well, what do you think about Alpha as a person? I happened to be his online e-girlfriend for a month.”

"Well, I guess he’s my personal favorite out of them all. He has good morals and he has a good job that makes him ample money,” he said in praise of Alpha, but then laughed at the notion of me being his e-girlfriend. “But in case you like him, you might face some tough competition. Almost all the female chat mates like him.”

"I think you must be confusing him with someone else. I am asking about Phantom, aka Alpha Male.”

Venom was quiet for a moment, probably thinking carefully about what he to say or perhaps considering whether or not there was even the most remote chance that it could be someone else.

“Huh, well girl, I guess anything is possible, but it would have to be a coincidence of epic proportions. I know this guy all too well and I can certainly guarantee that Phantom and Alpha Male are one and the same. His real name is actually Aaron and he’s been here for over a year now.”

I considered the chance that the Phantom that I knew might be a duplicate or something - or the likelihood that he finally showed his true character. "For some reason, I have a different opinion about Phantom, aka Alpha Male. He is a kinky, sex deprived man who dreams about sleeping with me all the time. You must be confused," I said with swagger.

"Doubtful. I believe that you are the confused one, Angel,” he said as we abruptly ended our call.

Admittedly, I realized that I didn’t even know Phantom’s real name. ‘Aaron, huh,’ I thought to myself. Then I dove into a pool of rage and anger once again. But before I let any of my thoughts turn into action, I decided to seek more information and speak with someone else who is friends with them. Surely Monica wasn’t an option. So, I laid my first bait.

“Rex, I am quite disappointed with you,” I scolded with a private message, “Someone just told me that you are friends with Cobra. Why didn't you tell me?”

"Hey now, I don't know much about him at all," Rex countered back.

"Well, do you think you can find something on him for me?" I pleaded.

Rex eagerly replied, "Sure."

I thanked him and we disconnected. I couldn't believe how caught up I was in my mission to set the story straight. It seems like the more I tried to solve this riddle, the more complicated it got. I questioned myself as to why I was even wasting my time on this bunch of guys, who apparently had nothing else to do in their lives. No job, no responsibilities and no family - they had nothing.

However, I had this feeling that I was leaving something unresolved - and I had something to say! I was going to get the last word in. Nobody tricks me and gets away with it. Phantom thinks that he is the smartest one, trying to trick people with his silly games. I wanted to confront him and let him know that I wasn't scared of his games. He can bring it on!

Meanwhile, I wanted to confront Cobra and his two aliases (Newguyintown and Notorious) to get their reactions. I searched for his ID and pinged him. My text went through, indicating that I was on his chat list. Bingo!

He responded pretty quickly and very crassly, "You are such a wild pussy!"

"Now Cobra, why would you call me a wild pussy? I expected gentlemanly behavior from you or I am out for good!"

"Fair enough - how about I call you Wild Cat? It will be between us. No one has to know about our dirty little secret."

"You have enough secrets on your plate, why do you wish to add more? For instance, you run a porn site, you are friends with Monica and Alpha aka Phantom - and you have my name, number, and location already. Last, but not least, I am your new target."

"Wow! You did your homework. I knew you are not a dumb, wild puss… I mean cat. You didn't disappoint me," he chided. "Yes, all of it is true, but I don't do it anymore. I have a business to run and I'm a very busy man. I am open to sharing my info with you to even the playing field. I know you own a business as well."

"Interesting. Carry on. Where are you and what do you do for living right now?"

"My name is Sam Baker. I live in New York and I import paper and plastic goods from China. I then sell these to wholesalers, newspaper agencies and other companies. I am telling you the truth and I won't say it again."

"Nice to meet you, Sam. I'm Tanya, but you already know that, don't you? So are you legal in this country?"

"Yes I am, but I wasn't born in the US."

“What do you want from me?” I inquired.

He cleared his throat and answered, “Nothing. Let’s just be friends and maybe meet up some time if I happen to be flying to your city.”

“I will think about it, but if I don’t talk to you, you will put my personal information out on Channel1. Is that the deal?”

“Wildcat, or should I just call you Tanya, I know that trick will not work with you, so I am not gonna do that. How about I promise you that I’ll never call you, but you can call me anytime you want. Or I will call you if you ask me to.”

“Okay whatever, but I’m going to talk to Phantom first. I will get back to you after I talk to him.”

“Oh, you mean Aaron - he is not coming back. You shouldn't wait on him, Wildcat,” he chuckled.

I pretended to disregard his comment and asked instead, “So what’s the reason you would want to run such a website and do this to innocent people?”

“I was young and stupid and I thought it was fun to play pranks.”

“Recording cam feeds without someone’s consent is not a prank, it’s illegal! You are intruding on someone's privacy.”

"Wildcat, do you really think these women are angels? Well, they aren't. Most of them are married or in committed relationships, yet they spend hours chatting and flirting, even doing cybersex with men online."

"Maybe so, but that still doesn't give you a reason to justify intruding on their privacy."

"Let me ask you this, Angel - you're from Tampa, Florida, right? I'm sure you've been to the beach and seen people in bikinis or thongs - maybe even making out. You've probably done some inappropriate things yourself. Have you ever been naked in public or done things to yourself that you shouldn't have done at the time? Now, what if you were in public and someone took a picture of you doing something like this. Would that be illegal? And if you think so, how do you police it? Bottom line is, don't do things in public that you don't want others to see - and don't share things online that you don't want everyone to see."

I didn't know how to answer that. Yes, he was right - you can't really stop people from taking pictures on the streets or in public - of whatever that could be: maybe a guy playing pocket pool and juggling his balls in his pants, or an innocent card game on the front porch of someone's house or people having a quickie in the back seat of a car. After a moment of silence, I heard him hang up on me. I don't like it when people walk over me, he should have at least said goodbye rather than just hanging up. Rude!

The next day, I was really busy at the gallery and I needed to focus on my work, but Sam's question kept resonating in my head. I was searching for a way to rationalize it, trying to find an appropriate answer. I needed to quiet the cacophony in my mind and get back to work. The gallery had finally signed a deal for an auction event and we had guests coming in from all across the United States. This was going to be a big event and I decided to do something different this time. We were not only providing accommodation for the guests, but food as well for the buyers who registered with us for a year. I cut down my profit margins from the sales and decided to spend the extra money to create a solid list of repeat buyers.

While I was going over our registered buyers list and familiarizing myself with their last purchases and the company evaluations, I got a call through iVoice from Sam. I wondered why he was calling me at this time of the day. He knows I must be at work. My mind started reeling as the phone rang again - could it be something urgent? Why would he be calling me - I am the last person who could help him. I sensed this strange love/hate feeling going on in my heart.

I finally picked up the call on what would certainly be the last ring before the app's voice messaging picked up. "Yes Sam, how can I help you?"

I could hear traffic in the background as he cheerfully greeted me, "How are you doing, my Wildcat?"

"I am doing fine. Why did you call me? I'm busy at work."

"I'm lost and I could really use your help. I need some directions to an address in New York. Are you on the computer? I'm at the airport in New York; can you please put this address into Google maps for me?"

I cut him off before he gave me that address, "Is this one of your tricks to somehow find my current location?"

"Wildcat, everything is not about you. Please get over it and help me. My 4G is not working on my phone right now and..."

He rambled on with some excuses before he finally gave me the address. Before I knew it, I was typing the info on Google maps - and bingo, I quickly found the directions he needed. He went on to tell me that he was in an Enterprise rental car, trying to get home. I couldn't understand why he didn't just take a cab, but before I could ask, he said he needed to go around the city after picking up someone.

I didn't understand him, nor did I need to. He's a fraud. I don't even know why I was helping him or even entertaining a conversation with him.

"I am about to meet your boyfriend," he said in a snide tone.

"My boyfriend? I don't have boyfriend, Sam," I retorted.

"You and Alpha, I mean Aaron, are together right?"

"No, we are not together. If you meet him, just tell him that I'm going to kill him with my bare hands. I am mad at him right now!"

He laughed in his sinister way, "I just recorded what you said. I think I utilized my 60 seconds of app recording time today in a good way!"

Unbelievable. This guy was incorrigible! "Are you freaking crazy or what? I didn't mean that I was going to literally end his life. Are you going to blackmail me over this? Go get a life! You need some serious help," I said with anger in my voice. I could feel my ear lobes turning red hot with anger and I started hyperventilating.

He let out another evil laugh, "I am not going to blackmail you. I [will] give this to Alpha, I mean Aaron!"

That made me lose my mind. I hung up on him and resolved to destroy both of these men. I had had enough of them playing games with me. They had no idea that they messed with the wrong person. I can be nice to a certain extent, but not to bullies and blackmailers. They needed to be put in their rightful place.

I wrapped up my important work at the gallery and headed home. While driving home through the rush hour traffic downtown, I replayed some options in my mind to get revenge. I considered going rogue so that I could collect as much information as possible on these three characters - Monica, Sam and Aaron. Then I could relay my information to the local authorities, although I wasn't sure whose jurisdiction this case would fall under. I knew that Sam was based in New York, but I was here in Tampa.

I remembered an old friend who had worked for the military in the past and was now working as a detective in the State of Florida. I called her and told her that something was going on with a friend of mine and asked her what she would suggest doing about it. She informed me that organized cybercrimes fell under the jurisdiction of the FBI, Federal court and Homeland Security. Finding out how to reach an agent at the FBI could be a challenge for me though. I really had no proof of any of this. After all, none of them had caused me any physical, mental, or financial harm yet - just emotional unrest. Although, he did breach my privacy without consent by unblocking my number. Then I thought about the website and the fact that he was harming other unsuspecting girls. I then got paranoid and thought, 'What if Sam and Aaron are tracking my phone and laptop?' I came to the realization that they might have already located my IP address and my physical location. Who knows, maybe they have some kind of remote app that lets them tap into my laptop.

I made a quick stop at Best Buy on the way home. Just to play it safe, I decided to buy a new laptop, hotspot and phone. I would use my new toys to gather more evidence on them so that I could reach out to the FBI with some solid evidence. I decided that it was imperative that they could not know that I was on to them. Sam and Monica's website needed to go away for good!

I thought that they might have been tracking my activities on Channel 1, therefore I couldn't be gone for too long and not log in to the app - that would make them suspicious. So when I got home, I logged in to Channel 1 and turned off my screen saver so that the computer wouldn't go into sleep mode. I wanted to make sure that I was online while I was working on setting up my new laptop and phone.

Stooping to their level and spying on these hooligans was unsettling for me - I couldn't believe the can of worms that I had opened. At this point, standing up to these bullies was the only right thing for me to do. I took a break from my covert operation to vent my feelings in a few lines of poetry:

Little did he know about her for sure
She was intrigued by stories of his lure
A silly little cupid stuck him hard
His ego crashed like a deck of cards
Fishing his heart out of a shallow lake of love
She was unwilling to be his dove
A knight from the south, a man with gold
Others with promiscuous desires they could not hold
Baffled by masquerade and pretentious care
Amour ended, not so fair love affair.

CHAPTER FIVE

The Conman "Cobra"

I checked my nose for cocaine residue in the rearview mirror as I sat momentarily at a red light in front of my destination. She did do well giving me the directions, but she is stupid, not thinking about the fact that someone could use her so easily. I could have been a terrorist or an assassin who was about to kill the president or blow up a building or even shoot someone. This naive girl helped a guy she hardly knows and she guided me through the city to an address she knows nothing about. Even if she searched for the address on Google maps, she wouldn't be able to find me; I was smart enough to give her my neighbor's location in the building across the street.

I parked the rental car, fetched my bags from the trunk and headed into my building. As I walked into the front lobby, I saw Aaron watching a football game at the front desk with the security officer. I motioned for him to follow me as I headed toward the elevators.

As we entered the elevator, I pushed button 18 for the penthouse level and I asked him, "So where are you with that girl?"

"It's done. The two of them are done," Aaron stated and then added, "I want to keep Tanya for myself - you can have her friend Dorothy."

I remained in silent thought as we entered the penthouse. I poured him a glass of bourbon and dropped an ice ball into it. This would be the best bourbon he has ever tasted in his life - now and for the future too.

As he took a sip of the bourbon, I broke my silence and said, "That was not the deal man. I gave you the file on Tanya, not Dorothy."

He winced slightly as he sipped the fine bourbon, "Tanya is beyond our scope, she is smart and intelligent, and she has very high morals."

"I know that. You don't have to teach me!" I snapped back at him.

"How would you know that? Did you talk to her?"

"Yes. She gave me a call. We have been talking over text and phone for a few days now."

He seemed shocked at my statement and quickly fired back, "That's not even remotely possible! She wouldn't have called you on her own. What did you do to her? Are you blackmailing her? Did you use the cam software on her?"

"Are you fucking crazy? She hates you," I said with a grin.

Aaron couldn't stand it any longer and he reached out to grab me, but I dodged his pathetic attempt to physically intimidate me.

"It's not possible!" he shouted. "She is mine. You stay away from her," he said with a finger raised to my eye level, as he lunged toward me to grab me by the shirt and pinned me against the wall. He was strong and well-built and I struggled to escape before kneeing him in the groin.

The pathetic fuck bent double and collapsed on the floor. I took advantage of his momentary incapacitation and grabbed my phone. If he thought the physical pain in his nuts was bad, I couldn't wait to dish out some even more poignant mental anguish as I clicked play on my phone's stored recording. Tanya's voice was loud and clear on the recording, "Phantom, no, we are not together. If you meet him, just tell him that I'm going to kill him with my bare hands. I am mad at him right now!"

His reaction was just as I had anticipated - swift and physical. He flexed his muscles, stood up straight in spite of his still-aching crotch, clenched his fists and charged right at me. I glanced over at my gun on the counter, but Aaron couldn't have cared less. I had unleashed a monster. The anger pumping through his veins was enough to break every bone in my body. He started to throw punches at me like a professional boxer, hitting me in the face, chest and abdomen. He hit me harder and harder, my bones cracked and my body contorted with pain. I tried to defend myself with my arms, but his punches overpowered me. He just wouldn't stop!

I could see in his enraged eyes that he was envisioning Tanya - and he was probably imagining me fucking her. I could tell that he was pissed that he lost both his women - first Monica, and now Tanya, to me! Now he was retaliating and trying to avenge his losses.

"Fuck you, you fucking con man. You fucking womanizer. You fucking asshole!" he shouted as he continued to pound on me.

I went limp for a minute as my body tried to recover from the blows it was taking. He sensed this and slowed his punches for a second, giving me an opportunity to counter with a homerun punch of my own, right to his jaw. Somehow, I managed to knock him down. I made a dash for the gun, grabbed it and clicked the safety off. I began firing wildly all over the penthouse. My aim was non-existent as my vision was obscured by the blood in my swollen eyes. Bullets whizzed in all directions, popping holes in my walls, furniture and appliances as I attempted to get him in the fire line of my gun, but he managed to dive behind the desk and evade my shots. I emptied the clip of all 11 of its 9mm bullets and quickly reached for the drawer to grab my backup clip. Aaron took advantage of the momentary cease-fire to try to make a dash for the door. I popped in the clip and fired in his direction.

He fell limp onto the floor, halfway between the couch and the front door. I staggered in agony from the pain of the beating that I had taken, dropping to my knees and shuffling across the floor. I grabbed my phone from the counter and held it in my trembling hand, swiping the screen feverishly to unlock the device. The blood on my fingers made it difficult, but the lock screen finally opened and I managed to hit the speed dial button that I needed.

"Answer bitch, answer!" I shouted at the ringing phone as blood dripped out of my busted mouth.

"Hello?" I was relieved to hear her voice on what seemed like the millionth ring.

"Monica," I said as I labored to speak.

"Sam, what's wrong? Are you okay?"

"No," I gasped.

"What the fuck happened?"

"I had a huge fight… with Aaron… he attacked me…" I stammered on my words as I glanced over at his body, lying on the floor in a pool of blood. "I… I… I fucking shot him…"

"What the fuck, Sam! Did you kill him?"

"I… I… don't know," I said as I stared at his back. He lay face down in a fetal position. "I'm hurt badly... possibly some broken bones... and maybe internal bleeding. I need you here right now. Now!"

"I will be on the next flight. Hang in there. Hide the body, then lie down and try to calm yourself down to slow your pulse and stop your own bleeding."

"Hurry, please... we have to… clean up… hide… drop bomb, recordings to Feds…"

"I'm on my way. Keep your phone close. I'll check in once I get to the airport. Hang in there, baby."

I wiped the blood from my eyes with my blood-stained shirt sleeve. I attempted to stand up with an intent to cautiously make my way over to him to see if he was breathing. I struggled to gain my footing as broken glass and shit crunched under my feet. I grabbed the corner of the counter and pulled myself up, but I slipped on my own blood on the slick tile floor as I took my first step and came crashing down onto the hard floor, head first. My ears rang and my vision narrowed into a tunnel as the sight of the body on the floor in front of me gave way to a white light… and then... nothingness.

~

I was only fourteen years old, living with my parents and five siblings in a very small flat in an insignificant town in a lesser known country. Like the rest of our town, we were dirt poor. I thought things were bad, but then they got much worse one night when my world was turned upside down. At dinner, my father addressed me and explained how he was going to disown me and ship me off to an orphanage so that my uncle could adopt me and ultimately move me to the United States with me so that I could have a better life.

I stared at the paltry offering of potatoes and some sort of potted meat on my plate as my father explained, "Son, I want a better future for you."

I looked up from my plate and looked my father in the eyes and pleaded, "My future is with my family and my friends. I want to go to school, but I want to go to school here."

My father choked back his shame and sternly said the obvious, "We have no money to send you to school."

"Send me to school and I will work to pay my way," I reasoned. "I can pay for their school too," I added, pointing to my little sister who was only four years old.

My father wasn't having it. He pounded his fist on the table and said, "Enough! We have already made arrangements for you. It will be much easier for you to succeed in America. You will earn dollars there, instead of pennies here."

I contained my emotion and continued my plea, "But... I will be so far away from you and everything that I know."

My father reached across the table, grabbed my hand and said, "I am sure you can make new friends there. After all, you will be with your own uncle and aunt."

"How much money do you need to keep me here and let me go to school here?"

"More than your fingers can count," He answered shamefully as his gaze dropped and focused on his empty plate.

"How can you do this to me?" I asked as tears welled up in my eyes.

"You will thank me later," he replied in a somber tone.

"I will spit on your grave, for doing this to your own child," I blurted out in anger.

My comment was met with a prompt slap across the face from my father's hand. I jumped up from the table and my father did the same. We were eye to eye and I stared at him defiantly. He raised his hand to slap me again, but my mother intervened and grabbed his arm before he could deliver another blow. I wanted him to hit me again. I needed him to hit me so that I could realize that this was real and that this was no longer my family.

Instead, he lowered his hand and leaned in towards me and then whispered in my ear, "You will thank me later, my boy."

And that was that. The next thing that I knew, I was enrolled at a home school program and living at an orphanage for the next two years. My uncle from the United States would come and visit me at the orphanage and bring me cool gifts from time to time. I didn't care very much about the books that he bought me. I could read, but I couldn't understand the characters and a lot of the details in the books. I hated my situation and the fact that I was still stuck in my country, but living in an orphanage away from my friends and family.

Then finally, just as he had promised, the day came when I could leave that shit hole and fly away to the beautiful new horizon that awaited me. The plan was for us to move to a big city near our town and stay in a hotel for about ten days when we first arrived. I was taught how to speak English and answer a few basic questions. I had to memorize the contact details and address of my uncle and aunt, Mr. and Mrs. Baker. Unfortunately, they became my new mom and dad and they changed my name from Nick to Sam. When the adoption was finalized, I emerged as Sam Baker.

It really sucked at first because by the age of 16, I had already had three sets of parents and three different names. My birth parents and birth name, Nick, had all but faded into oblivion as my guardian 'parents' at the orphanage had called me everything under the sun, except for my real name. Now my paternal uncle and aunt were my parents and my new name, Sam, signified a new beginning for me, or so I assumed.

Before we departed for the USA, my uncle and aunt, excuse me, my parents, took me shopping for some essentials. At the airport, I was handed this small, green booklet that I was instructed not to lose because I would have to show it to these men in uniform before I could enter the airport and board the plane. I stood in a long line and eagerly awaited seeing my first airplane up close, in person. I had only seen them fly overhead from a distance. The line moved up slowly, one person at a time, but after meeting with the men in uniform, I finally was able to get to the part of the airport where I could see the huge airplane. I couldn't have ever imagined the size of the plane and was equally surprised that they could fit so many people inside of it at once. I guess I was hoping to have a plane all to myself, like in some American movie that I had once watched.

We waited for what seemed like an eternity as I stared out of the window at the plane and wondered about the physics of how it actually flew. Then, after an hour or so, this lady at the desk started calling out numbers on the intercom. Everyone stood up and we walked down this long bouncy hallway and into to the airplane. I squinted as I peered into the plane because it was bright as daylight inside. I handed my only bag to my uncle and he put it in a cabinet overhead and then pointed and motioned for me to sit. The seats were very comfortable, but my knees touched the seat the front of me. I didn't know what to do, so I asked my uncle if I could have the aisle seat, in order to be able to spread my legs out more. I was immediately disappointed with my decision because I realized that I wouldn't be able to see out of the window anymore. My disappointment vanished however, as I soon realized that the windows didn't open anyway.

The plane began to move and soon it started to make a loud noise and move much faster. My ears popped and my stomach felt like it was floating, but I soon got used to the feeling. I tried to sleep on the plane, but it got very cold at night and the cold air hit me in the face all night. I had to pee, so I used my newly learned English and asked the lady in the pretty dress for the restroom. She directed me to the rear of the plane, but I asked her to accompany me and she obliged.

She opened the door to the bathroom, which looked more like a closet, and showed me how to lock the door once I went inside. I wish that she had showed me where to pee. I stood there looking around until I couldn't hold it in any longer. I decided that the sink must be the place to relieve myself. I stood, tiptoed and emptied my bladder into the sink, then ran cold water into it to wash it down. I looked around, but I couldn't find a towel to dry it off. I did find a roll of white paper, but it shredded into small pieces when I tried to tear it off. My penis ended up looking like a sausage with white breadcrumbs on it! Then came a knock on the door.

"Sir, are you alright?" the lady in the nice dress asked through the door.

I shoved my penis back into my pants and answered, "Yes, I am done!" I fumbled to open the door and then quickly returned to my seat.

I finally fell asleep and didn't wake up until we landed. After countless hours of traveling in the airplane and then in a car, we were about to reach our new home; however, much to my disappointment, we stopped at a hotel instead. My uncle got out and took all of my belongings out of the car. My aunt remained sitting in the car and looked away, avoiding eye contact with me. I just knew that she didn't like me already. My uncle carried my bag and summoned me to cross the parking lot with him. I followed him inside through a rotating door. I couldn't believe my eyes - it was big inside! I stood in the middle of the lobby and watched my uncle talk to another man in a suit. Periodically, this man would glance over at me as if to inspect me from head to toe.

My uncle motioned for me, "Sam, come here. This is where you will live and this man is going to tell you what to do."

I was shocked and scared as I said, "I thought I was going to stay with you."

My uncle pulled me by the elbow close to him and then leaned down to my level, "Get this straight, your father sent you here to work so that you could send money back home to them. Think of your siblings, Sam."

"Yes, but he said I would be staying with you."

"Ha!" he scoffed. "As if your father could afford that. He kept you in the dark, boy."

My lip quivered and my hands got sweaty. "No, he wouldn't do that do to me," I said as my voice cracked. "You promised my dad that you would bring me here to get an education for my future."

"I promised him money that he will get each month," he answered with no remorse. "You better get to work. Don't act smart. I will keep your passport and other documents," he said as he fetched my little green book and a couple pieces of paper from my bag.

"Where will I sleep and what will I eat? What about my school?" I asked as I stood shaking with fear in the middle of the hotel lobby.

"You are old enough to figure everything out."

"Where can I reach you? Just in case I need you."

"You have our number. See, it's here in your bag."

"How can I call my parents?"

"I will give you a phone next time we meet."

"When? What about my school?"

"Yes, we will figure that out in a month or so. Now go and have a look around with this man," he said as he ushered me closer to the hotel manager.

He waved goodbye to me and the hotel manager and without another word, he turned and walked out of the revolving door.

I was perplexed and had no idea what to expect and what was going to happen with my future. I decided to man-up and do what needed to be done. After all, I thought to myself, any lifestyle would be better for me than the orphanage. So I followed the manager through the hotel as he gave me a tour. He pointed out various spots that I could settle down in and told me that I could choose anywhere that I liked - as long as it wasn't in any of the guest rooms or offices. I walked through the entire property a couple of times and found my spot near the rear of the building where there was a beautiful hallway.

I soon realized over the next couple of days that I had made a bad choice with regard to my living quarters. The music from the banquet hall would go on for hours after midnight on weekends and reverberated through my room. On weekdays, it was much quieter though. At least when there were parties, I would get to have a feast those weekends. At other times, I just got to eat regular American food (which was still better than what I was accustomed to). Within a week or so, I packed up my bags and moved closer to the kitchen into a storage room, right next to the catering office. It was much quieter there, with the exception of occasional intrusions for stocking and clearing out supplies. I managed to make friends with the staff and they did my laundry for free. Sometimes, they would even sneak me in for a quick shower in the guest rooms between check-in and cleaning.

I worked hard and did well. As a reward, I was promoted from janitor to a waiter at the big hall at the rear of the hotel.

After a month, my uncle finally stopped by to visit and was quite pleased with my work. My eyes twinkled as he patted me on the back and told me that he was proud of my accomplishments so far. Since he was happy and praising me, I thought it would be a good time to hit him up for something, so I asked him if I could buy myself a rug for my bed because it had started to get cold at night. His facial expression changed quickly from pleasure to disappointment and he said, “Sam, we don't have enough money to pay for luxury like that. What do you want - a bed or to go to school?”

My choice was obvious and I answered, slightly dejected, “I would like to go to school.”

To cope with the cold nights of the oncoming winter, I decided to move to a different part of the hotel where it was warmer at night. I chose the warmest place in the whole building - the boiler room! A month later, my uncle visited again, and again I asked him for the rug, but again he simply shook his head in disapproval of my request.

I countered this time with a question more in line with my real motive, "Okay, but can I at least have a copy of my US passport?"

My question was met with his question, "Why do you need that?"

"I want to enrol in a school and there are activities and after school classes. I think they said some of my documents are missing. Could you just stop by my school?"

He seemed annoyed that I would ask that of him and he replied, "I don't have time to do all that. I will give you a copy. Just give it in the school office yourself."

I was delighted that he took the bait. He made a copy, which I took, but he kept the original.

I was so excited to finally be able to enrol myself in school, but I figured I would have to work harder or get another job at the hotel or even at the school. I couldn't ask for favors at the school, as most of the teachers were already spending extra time tutoring me and some of them had even chipped in money on my books.

My mother would always say, “A mother feeds the baby, when he cries,” meaning that no one would help me unless I asked for it. So I started to ask around for extra work to earn extra cash. I told them that I needed money for a bed and a rug and maybe some more clothes and other basic things. The laundry guy at the hotel was gracious enough to offer an old box spring mattress and sheets that the hotel was disposing off anyway.

“What do you want boy?” the laundry man asked.

I was ecstatic as I looked through the pile of junk. “Everything!” I said with excitement, my eyes wide open and my mind reeling with all the options I had to choose from.

“Now wait, you can’t take all of this at once,” he said to temper my excitement.

“Oh,” I said with a tone of disappointment.

“Maybe take a few things now and then take a few more things later next month. So, what do you want first?” he asked as we perused through the junk pile.

“I want the mattress and the rug,” I answered confidently.

“You mean the comforter? This thing?” he said holding up the thing that I had been referring to as a bed rug.

“Yes, that comforter, please. I was excited to finally get the cover for the bed and to learn a new word in the process.

"How about a pillow?"

"No thank you, I am good," I answered in shame of taking too much at first.

"Boy, go on and take it now - I might not offer it to you again. Now let me help you get these to your room," he said, dusting off my newfound items.

We loaded everything onto a cart and slowly start moving towards my quarters. I was praying that we wouldn't pass the hotel manager, but just when we were a few steps away from the kitchen, I saw him walking in our direction.

"What are you doing with all this trash?" he asked.

"Nothing, sir," I answered.

The laundry man chimed in to back me up, "He is just helping me get these to the dumpster."

"Whatever, just use the rear hallway and don't parade the trash through the main lobby," the manager ordered.

"Sure thing, we will do that," I replied.

"What are you so excited about anyway?" he asked as he could see that I was way too happy to be simply making a trash run to the dumpster.

I contained my emotion and simply said, "Nothing, sir."

Since I now had a comforter to keep me warm, I decided to move from the boiler room back into the panty near the kitchen. We dragged the mattress and my other items quickly through the kitchen and into my old quarters in the pantry room. I then sat my 'new' mattress down on the floor, dove onto it and laughed my guts out. I was as happy as a child on Christmas morning! I had the best night's sleep I think I'd ever had in my life that night.

I managed to find another part-time job at a nearby gas station, just a three mile walk from the hotel. I would sneak out and work there alternating nights. In a few months, I was able to find and rent an apartment of my own; however, my uncle refused to sign the paperwork, so that didn't pan out. Instead, I was able to negotiate a twin bedroom at the hotel for myself. Life was much better after six months of living in more proper conditions. Plus, it was summer already and I got a break from school, which allowed me more time to work and earn more money. I never quit working at the gas station. It was my first job and the owner was very supportive. I wanted to stay loyal to him because I considered him to be a true father figure - a far cry from my real father, the orphanage guardian, my uncle or the hotel manager.

It was a chilly, clear night and I was working the late shift at the gas station. It seemed like a very normal, mundane night, but little did I know that this was the night that I would remember for a very long time. This night, during my shift at the gas station, the owner of the gas station stopped by.

He had made a surprise visit and came by to say hi to me. "Yo ho, kid! How are you doing?" he announced as he cheerfully strolled through the front swinging glass door of the store.

I smiled like a child who had just spotted Santa Claus and I greeted him with, "I am doing great, Sir."

"How is your school? You play football or basketball?"

"No sir, I just study," I answered with pride.

"Well, your studying is really paying off. Your English is getting much better."

"Yes, my teachers are helping me a lot."

"Keep your hands off the girls. They will suck the life out of you," he cautioned.

"No, no," I chuckled.

"I am telling you! Just focus on your study groups and not the boobs," he said as he patted me on the back.

We both burst into laughter, but our fun quickly faded as a bunch of thug looking guys walked into the store and headed toward the restroom. One of the guys stood next to the drink section while talking on his cell phone. I made my way over to that area and pretended to organize some shelves while the owner stayed at the register. We had had a lot of shoplifters recently, so I wanted to keep a close eye on them.

The dude on the phone immediately moved closer to the register as if to avoid me. He began pacing back and forth at the front of the store and looked at the old man behind the register. I wondered if he knew him or something. As I was trying to figure out what he was doing and why he was so anxious, the other men stepped out of the restroom together and proceeded to march toward the register. I could see the owner doing something behind the counter with a sense of urgency. It turns out, he was emptying the register into the safety deposit box.

In an instant, all four men drew guns from under their hooded sweatshirts and pointed them at the owner and demanded the cash. It all happened so fast that I froze and my mind went blank as time slowed down in this surreal moment.

"Give me the cash," the guy in black hoodie shouted.

He kept repeating the same command and looked at his watch many times as if he was in some kind of time bomb and the clock was ticking. He brandished his gun in the face of the owner as one of the guys stood guard at the door and the other two filled their pockets with items from the shelves. I slouched down only few feet away from them, trying to hide myself from these goons. Every ounce of me wanted to help the old man, but with each ticking second I moved in slow motion, almost as if I was frozen in time. My mind reeled as I realized that I would be of no help, so I began planning my escape through the rear end of the store.

The old man looked the thug in the eyes, as he secretly pulled out his gun while opening the cash register. In the back of my mind, I knew what was coming. The old man broke his eye contact with the thug and looked over at me. He nodded his head in approval one last time and I could read his final thoughts in his eyes. As he drew the gun from behind the counter and raised it toward the thug, I took off running to the back of the store and I heard the first shot fired. I heard the flying shots as I ran through the stock room and out of the back door. In my mind, I played over and over again how these men could shoot holes in such an innocent man's life.

I just ran, and ran, and ran while screaming and crying for help.

A few days later, I returned to the gas station, which was now sealed as a crime scene. I looked at the store from across the parking lot. From there, I had a painful vantage point of what a shattered dream looked like. I wondered what would happen to the old man's family and kids.

Life went on without so much as a hiccup. Within a month, there was new ownership and the store was back in business like nothing had ever happened. It was very difficult and it would never be the same, but I returned to my job working nights at the gas station. I pondered what would have happened that night if the old man hadn't popped in to see me. Maybe he would still be alive and I would be the one six feet under. I thought to myself that I needed to man up as I was now a potential target since I had seen the men who did the shooting.

After my first shift back at the store, I went home and took a long, hot shower. I looked at my scrawny body in the bathroom mirror and realized that it was clearly no good for self-defense. I needed to have a weapon - or needed to join a gang or something so that I would have protection and these kids would have no reason to retaliate against me.

I decided to venture through the city to find the old man's family or friends. I couldn't find them, but I came to terms with the fact that therc was so much poverty and discontent in the city in which I lived. It was nowhere near as bad as back in my home country, but still so many people needed a place to live or a job or decent education. I started to feel much more fortunate about my situation, so I decided to try to do some good to counter this bad situation.

I began to supply sheets, mattresses, pillows, and toiletries at minimal costs to these underprivileged kids. On weekends, we had large gatherings at the hotel and it was easy to steal food. I justified my theft because a hell of a lot of food would go waste anyway. While taking the trash out, I would wrap the meat and bread in bags and hide it in the trash can, and my underprivileged friends would pick it up from dumpster. I continued this for many days to come.

I was soon to be eighteen, and I had been preparing myself for this landmark birthday. I decided to quit my job at the hotel and move into an apartment in Midtown. I traveled to DC and filed for a new passport to replace the one that my uncle was holding hostage. I also obtained a driver's license and was beginning to feel like a very independent young man. I was ready for college!

In just about a year, I was able to save seven figures from the website's profits. I always wanted to be my own boss and have the money and power to do something for the old man's family. I often reminisced about how he had been a good role model and an ideal father figure to me. I went back to the gas station and spoke with the manager who was able to put me in contact with the new owners.

I visited one of the owners and made him an offer to purchase the gas station. I was able to negotiate a price which was $25,000 over their purchase price just a year prior. It was a quick profit for them and a new business venture for me. I applied for a commercial bank loan for commercial property. After I made the $50,000 down payment, I still had a considerable amount of money in my bank account as a security blanket and cushion. Unlike the website, I wanted this business venture to be legit and something that I could be proud of. I opened my own business bank account, hired a staff and set up my new office. I had this overwhelming feeling that I was doing something good.

I never forgot the old man and thought about his family and kids often. After much research, I was able to locate the cemetery in which he was buried. I decided to visit his grave and pay my respects to him with some flowers. I attempted to find his wife and kids, but through the rumor mill I learned that the wife had moved away to an unknown city and that his kids were in colleges in other cities as well.

Nobody really seemed to care but me. My uncle no longer visited me or even answered my calls. The hotel had a change in management and a new staff took over. I came to the realization that the world was constantly changing, it stopped for no one. It's a crude world out there and the harsh reality therein made me sad and depressed at times. I became disenchanted with the gas station as it caused me to dwell on the negative memories. I thought it was going to be a positive venture in my life, but I was wrong, so I decided to man up and get rid of the things and people in my life who were holding me back. The first thing I did was to sell the gas station. I decided to start fresh with a new business, so I bought a UPS store. I had heard it was a good investment with no drawbacks and most importantly, no emotional history attached to it.

Despite the new business and its immediate success, I still felt the same way and was uncertain what to do about it. I considered making an even more drastic change and moving out of the city to start over completely fresh somewhere else altogether.

Chapter Six

The Meltdown

I found myself engaging in activities that were against my morals and values - things that I would normally never do. Every time that I crossed over a personal boundary, I found myself pushing to just go for it. I wondered how far I could go and if it would forever change me and ruin my existence and reputation that I had worked so hard to build over the last twenty-plus years. I had to think not only about myself, but my business and family as well. I considered whether people would question my judgment or family values or core ethics - and whether or not it was worth the risk to me.

I once read how a guru described three different kinds of people in the world. First, there were the ones who are smart enough to understand right and wrong and the direction necessary in order to achieve a goal. Next, there were the kind of people who needed to be taught and required guidance as to what needs to be done to get the desired result. Lastly, there are the ones who needed someone to literally force them into find their way. For some of those in the third category, we have correctional facilities, where individuals are forced to come to grips and to realize and analyze that what they did was wrong.

I would speculate and debate that the term 'wrong' is subjective. I agree with that. What's wrong to me may be right to someone else and vice versa.

Humans are social animals who believe in the popular opinion of the collective society. The opinion that is not popularly accepted, is often considered as 'wrong'. The individual morals and ethics are sometimes taught or learned at a smaller scale, say at the level of family or community. I remember when I was growing up; it was completely okay to use words like "stupid" or "idiot" in conversations at my friends' homes. When my mom complained to my kindergarten teacher about other kids in my class using these words, the teacher simply replied that it was something that was acceptable in that particular kid's home and the school had no authority over that. She went on to explain to my mother how the teachers discouraged the use of these words at school. Little did my mom know that *my* friends didn't utter such words when the teachers were around.

I digressed from the conversation and I am deviating from the point I'm trying to make - which happens often with me; one topic leads to another and then to the third one and so forth.

I was very aware that I could simply walk away from this online mess and enjoy the life that my father had dreamed of for me - or I could stand up for what I believe is right and put an end to what's been wrong for so many years. I was sure that some might have tried and lost the battle in the past, but in my heart and soul, I knew it was time to march together and put an end to this.

On that note, I picked my phone and dialed up my detective friend Stephanie again. This time I planned to be very truthful with her and explain the situation entirely. I would come clean and tell her that it happened to me rather than a friend of mine, as I had previously stated on our last call.

The phone rang and rang before I left her a voicemail message, "Hey, this is Tanya! How are you doing? I need your help. I have something going on and it's kind of urgent. If you could give me a call that would be great. Thank you. Bye!"

About five minutes after hanging up the phone, she called me back.

"Hey Tanya," she said.

I made a little small talk and chit chat to catch up on personal history as well as to quell my nerves. "Hey Stephanie! How are you doing? I see you are engaged now."

"Yes, I finally got a good man. He is on active duty in the military right now."

"Nice! Well, congratulations. When is the big day?"

"Sometime next year. We haven't quite decided on the date yet. So enough about me, what made you call me? What's going on and how can I help?"

I confessed that I was in trouble and told her everything that was happening on the iVoice app. I also told her how I had been working under a clone ID to obtain more information on these three troublemakers. She didn't say much at first, she just listened, but then at the very end she replied, "Let me look into this, but before we open up this can of worms, I want to know whether or not you are ready to file charges and proceed with the case?"

I didn't have to think at all before I replied, "Yes."

"Are you ready to come to court for rest of your life?"

"Yes."

"Are you prepared to pay for an attorney?"

Again, I quickly answered, "Yes."

"Great! I will get to work on this. Can you come to the station and fill out some paperwork? I would like to promptly start an official investigation. Meanwhile, I will try to pull out more information on the three of them and the dating app."

"Can I come today after lunch?" I eagerly asked.

"Great, I will see you soon."

I quickly checked in with Mrs. Martha to see if she could handle the meetings at the gallery for the rest of the day. I did my best to multitask and take as many phone calls as I could. My first auction was just two weeks away. I had the auction list in my possession and all the artifacts were scheduled to arrive this week. I had to increase the security at the gallery, so I hired additional staff for that purpose. I was using state of the art servers to keep the security cameras running in case of power outage. I also had more power generators installed to back up the servers. I brought in two additional guards to monitor the cameras. Not only did I have the auction list ready, but all of the potential buyers were locked in as well. The buyers list stayed locked in the safe with some of the other auction items. The accommodation information and the auction item catalogue had already been both emailed and mailed to the buyers. Everything was shaping up nicely. I couldn't go wrong on this one!

After a quick pit stop for lunch at the local sub shop, I rushed my way to the police station. I really couldn't remember the last time, if ever, that I was at a police station. While driving my way through the traffic, I recalled the episodes from a Netflix series that I used to watch. I reached this old brick building which almost looked like a courthouse from the 1970's. The building was one story high and very simple in design and appearance. I assumed that I was at the right place because the parking lot was filled with police cars and unmarked government vehicles. I parked my car at the rear of the parking lot and walked towards a small building on which there was a sign that read "Police Department." I had a pit in my stomach as I made the trek across the parking lot. I knew that there would be no turning back from what I was about to start.

The place was narrow and not easily accessible; I almost bumped into a few strong built men who were exiting as I entered. The grey floor and an overbearing load of tables, chairs and lockers made the station even less inviting. I didn't expect the Ritz Carlton, but I guess the police department doesn't have to be a very inhospitable place. I walked up to a covered window with a small slot to speak through, much like an old bank teller window. The lady (and I use that term lightly) who was sitting at the desk behind the window, was busy thumbing through some files. She seemed bothered as I walked up, leaned over and asked for detective Stephanie Owens. She hardly even looked up from her paperwork and simply pointed me towards the office of the deputy sheriff.

I turned in the direction of her pointed finger and headed across the lobby. I took a deep breath and couldn't help but notice that the place smelled like a thrift store. With each stride across the grey tiled floor towards her office, I exhaled a sigh of relief that my dilemma would soon be over. I knocked on the door next to the placard labeled "Detective Stephanie Owens."

A stern female voice commanded from behind the closed door, "Please wait outside."

My enthusiasm turned into curiosity as I took a step back, just far enough so that I was still able to hear some men mumbling inside the room with her. It only took a moment for Stephanie to step out and wave her hand, motioning for me to get inside the room. I scanned the room to find two other officers who were both dressed in suits, but I didn't see badges on either one of them. They looked like they were straight out of the movie "Men in Black." Stephanie promptly introduced the two men to me as FBI agents. I was very nervous and intimidated by the whole process - particularly the whole air of secrecy those men were giving off.

One of the agents broke the silence and got right to the point, explaining that there have been multiple ongoing cases against the exact same app for almost a decade. The cases ranged from missing persons to sex trafficking, child pornography and many others. Due to the lack of evidence, the app is still up and running. If they are able to link a New York gang to the app, it would become easy for them to push many of the cases forward in the federal court.

"So how do I fit in?" I asked.

They implied that I would be working in conjunction with the FBI and Homeland Security. They went on to explain that they would pose as a pest extermination company to get into my house for surveillance. They planned to wire my entire house, tap all of my phones and place bugs throughout my house on a few of my gadgets. I would be responsible for getting either Sam or Aaron to confess about the website and their involvement with it.

"What happens after that? After you have recorded them confessing?" I asked.

The taller agent spoke up and reassured me, "We will take care of the rest, you don't have to worry about a thing."

I wanted to believe them, but I still had my concerns, so I asked, "What if they try to harm me or my business in anyway?"

"We can relocate you and provide you safety under the witness protection program," the shorter agent answered.

"I can't go into hiding, I have no one to take care of my family business," I said with tears welling up in my eyes as I fully comprehended the gravity of the alternative.

"This is the right thing to do and time is ticking. Every minute counts right now because they hop from one target to another in no time. If they lose interest in you, our case is pretty much over," the taller agent explained.

I thought for a minute as Stephanie and the two suits stared at me. I knew what I should do, but somehow it was still a terrifying decision. I took a deep breath and swallowed the lump in my throat as I said, "Okay. Let me arrange a few things with my personal assistant, Mrs. Martha. You can come next week to install the surveillance equipment in my house."

"I am sorry, Tanya! It has to been done today or tomorrow," the tall agent informed me.

"Alright. Tomorrow it is," I confirmed, knowing that I would have a lot to do in preparation and not a lot of time to do it.

I flashed a smile at Stephanie as I turned and exited her office. As I walked towards my car, my mind went numb and I couldn't think straight. I had thoughts of my auction items, buyer list, Sam, Aaron, and the FBI - all running together at the same time. I just wanted to break down and let out my tears and screams. I was so sick of having to act all grown up all the time; I wasn't sure if I could do it anymore. I wished I could just go back in time and re experience the innocence of childhood. I wanted to get away from all these social, moral, and familial responsibilities. I drove home and thought about what I would have for my last meal in peace and privacy before all the drama and surveillance started.

I parked my car and walked through the front yard towards the door. As I rummaged through my bag in search of my keys, my mind drifted to a thought of a situation from a movie I once saw, in which the female lead actor is being followed and was spooked by a man in a mask. Just then, I looked back to see if someone was following me. I looked left and right, and then down the street. Nothing and no one was there - not even a rumbling or a leaf falling off of a tree. No birds were chirping and no crickets were making noise. It was just eerily quiet!

Quickly, I shoved my keys back in my bag and flung the front door open. The door closed behind me as I rushed to the kitchen, dropped my things on the counter and flipped my sandals on the floor. I perused my fridge and found only some strawberries which I ate, and then drank some milk right out the carton. Before rushing to my bed, I made sure that I got rid of the duplicate laptop, the 'burner' phone and my spy IDs. I couldn't remember whether or not I had mentioned to the FBI officers that I had been spying on Sam and Aaron.

I could hear the clock ticking as the AC unit kicked off and on, periodically. These rhythmic sounds made me sleepy, but the thoughts in my mind were raising my anxiety.

I was zoning in and out of sleep, but slumber was alluding me. It was 3 AM as I checked the clock for the millionth time.

Finally, when I could see daylight out of my window, I got out of my bed and got all dolled up for the big day at work. As I traced my lips with pink lipstick, I heard the doorbell ring twice. I peered out of the window and saw the Zigzag Pest Control van parked out in front of my house. I took a deep breath and opened the door to find two men standing there in orange coveralls. They introduced themselves as exterminators as they walked in and closed the door behind themselves.

"So, are you planting something?" I asked.

One of the men interrupted me and said, "We will take care of everything ma'am, please just sit down and relax. Let us survey the house to find the source of the rodent infestation."

The man raised his eyebrows longer than required and put his finger to his pursed lips, indicating for me to stay quiet and not utter a word. They turned the entire house upside down as they looked for wiretaps, bugs and what not. I understood that these men meant business based on their demeanor. One of the guys indicated to the other that the house was clean. They even checked my laptop, TV and phone. Thank God it was all clean!

It took them another three hours to plant all of their bugs and establish connections to my laptop in such a way that they could monitor it from their system. With no goodbyes and no further instructions, they just left.

I called Stephanie to ask her what I should do for the next move.

She responded in a very curt, but professional manner, "Just do what they asked you to do - and don't worry, we are on your side."

She hung up abruptly. I felt like I was on my own. I decided to deal with this after I was done with my routine check at the art gallery. I realized that my priority needed to be worrying about the buyer list that day and not the surveillance at my home. After all, the buyers were coming into town the next week. I had to confirm a few more accommodations and it was already half past three. The day was slipping away from me.

I rolled into the gallery and greeted my assistant. "Hi Mrs. Martha, good morning - I mean good afternoon - actually, late afternoon - um, good early evening," I finally corrected myself and dialed into the right time.

Martha stared at me blankly and simply said, "Miss Tanya, there is an addition to the buyer's list."

I thought for a moment and then replied, "I think we are done adding buyers to our list, aren't we full for the auction?"

"Miss, I already did the background check for this buyer. He seems to be the right fit; he's young, rich and has great taste in art."

"You know best, Mrs. Martha. I trust you on this! What is his name?" I inquired.

"Let me see," Mrs. Martha said as she flipped through some pages in a folder. I felt like snatching the paperwork away from her hand and reading it myself. I found myself losing patience with everything!

"He is Mr. Nick Baker from New York City," Mrs. Martha proudly announced, finally.

"I have never heard of him before. When is he coming in?" I asked.

"Monday," she answered.

"Monday it is, then."

I promised Mrs. Martha that I would include this new buyer on the accommodation list. She took off for the day, and I remained in the office and checked the vault, security cameras, and the lists. In no time, it was midnight and I was about to crash on my office couch. I was too lazy to drive home - I just wanted to stay and check the app on my laptop. For a moment, I debated with myself whether to login from the office or not, but then I realized that that the FBI bugs were not set up on the Mac that I was using at the office. I considered what could happen if some hackers or Sam or Aaron hacked into my security system or got into my vault. I couldn't risk all that. "Gosh, what have I got myself into", I thought.

I took another hour to pack my belongings and then headed home. Maggy was waiting for me to take her out for her final walk for the day. As she jumped on my leg, I bent down to pet her and she licked my face. I got a creepy vibe as if someone was watching me from a distance, but I assured myself that is was just the men in uniform.

I sat down on my couch, popped open my laptop and began surfing through different channels on iVoice. Then Venom pinged me. Both Aaron and Sam were offline so I decided to chit chat with Venom for a while.

“Hey Venom, how are you doing? Long time, no see,” I said into the mic on my computer.

“Hey Iron Angel! Are you good? You haven’t been active on Channel 1 recently. Is it Phantom or is it Cobra who’s been keeping you busy lately?” he asked sarcastically.

“I guess they are taking turns making a fool out of me,” I answered in jest.

“You are letting it happen to you,” Venom said somewhat sympathetically.

“I am letting what happen to me? I mind my own business on here and I am not probing into other people's’ business. I don’t do any hanky panky stuff. I am not part of any groups or cliques. So, what am I doing wrong here?” I asked with frustration in my voice.

“They are messing with your head and wasting your time, because you are letting them. Just block both of those jerks and be done with them. Don’t be addicted to chat.”

"Don't get me started. I am not addicted to this app or to Phantom or Cobra or whatever. I can't wait to get over this app and I'm just waiting for a big thing to happen," I answered in my own defense.

"Yeah, all of us say that we are not addicted, yet we all have been here for a decade, more or less."

I rolled my eyes at the thought of being on the app for a whole decade before I responded, "Watch me - I am gonna shut this place down!" I smiled with satisfaction at my statement.

Venom laughed out loud and said, "You need to relax. Don't take this app too seriously. It's just online dating and it's only for fun!"

"Yea, well, I am all heated up right now. Is bullying, blackmailing or mocking someone fun to you? This online world is merely a representation of the real world; however, in real life there are more laws, while this place has almost none. Anyone can say or do anything, and most people seem to not care how much they hurt the other person. It's too easy to just type in some hateful stuff and get away with it."

"Girl, take a deep breath and forget about it," Venom tried to reason with me.

I fired back, "No, I am not going to calm down. I am done with this BS. Are you trying to tell me that no users and no conversations have ever affected you? You have felt absolutely no change in your personality over the last decade after using this app? Is that so? I can say I have never been this temperamental and nothing has ever offended me to the point that I plan to get revenge or cause harm to a person. I can feel the rage in my veins and my brain is gonna burst open with all the thoughts churning inside my head at warp speed."

"What revenge are you talking about?" Venom asked with a curious tone in his voice.

"Forget it! Nothing at all."

"Look, don't do anything stupid. I am telling you again, don't take this app too serious. It's just a place for people to chat and kill their time online."

"They shouldn't be doing it at the cost of others' feelings. Users like me are not here to entertain others at the cost of our privacy or emotions."

"You are way too sensitive for the online world," Venom stated bluntly.

"What's wrong with being sensitive?" I asked.

"Nothing is wrong with it, this is just not the place for you."

"This is not the place for anyone. Watch me shut this thing down," I blurted out before thinking.

"You are scaring me with your claim of shutting this down."

"I have reached out to my friend who is working with FBI. We are going to close this app and take down the perpetrators who are bullying others," I affirmed with certainty.

There was a long, awkward pause. I realized that I shouldn't have revealed that.

Venom broke the silence after a few moments and said, "All I can say is you are taking this way too seriously. It's not required for you to take matters into your own hands."

"I think I am done here. I can't say any more," I said as I ended the chat.

I changed into my gym clothes and ran out of the house to release some pent-up energy and clear my head. While I was running down the road towards a nature trail in the woods, I heard my phone ring! It was Sam calling.

"Hey Sam," I said as I answered the call.

"You seem to be out of breath. Is it because you are so happy that I called?"

"I am in the woods trying to run my way back home. I can't hear you very well, we have poor reception." There was silence on the other end of the phone. "Hello?" I said to see if he was still there.

I looked at my phone and there were no signal bars. I dropped his call and decided to run back home as fast as I could to call him from there. As soon as I got home, I made sure my laptop, TV and phone were all switched on and powered up. I wanted to guarantee that the FBI would capture the conversation I was about to have.

I was nervous. I bit my lip and dug my fingernails into my leg as I dialed his number. As the phone rang, I took a deep breath and tried to relax as he answered the phone. "Hey, sorry about that. I couldn't hear a thing, but I'm back home now."

He hesitated before responding, "Something is odd about you. You are being super nice to me this evening."

"Well, you are right. I'm in a good mood, but I've been trying to reach Aaron as I haven't heard from him. It's been a really long time since I last talked to him. Didn't you say that you were about to meet up with him?"

"Huh. It's always about Aaron. Are you in love with him?"

"No, I am not. It's just that I want to clarify a few things with him before we move forward."

"What? Move forward with him? Are you serious?"

"Move forward, um, I mean talk further." I tripped over my words a little from nervousness.

"Aaron, he is not going to talk to you anymore."

"And why is that?"

“He is not coming back. You two are done. You need to get over him,” he said in a snide tone.

“And what, get on to you now? Is that what you intend?”

“You are smart after all, my Wildcat.”

“I am *your* Wildcat now? So you can add me as a trophy on your prestigious website? I have checked that website,” I said as I attempted to bait the hook.

He defensively responded, “This is the last time we are talking about that website. As I said, we made it for fun; it’s not something that I wish to own for life.”

“We? Who else is with you? Monica? Aaron? And?...” I asked as I lured him into my trap.

“Just the three of us. No one else.”

“Well, when do you plan to close it?”

“It's not my place to make that decision. I co-own the site, but the revenue comes to my account. I may have to dispose of some things and people before shutting it down. It won't be easy.”

“What do you mean by disposing of people?”

“I just have to push them away from my life - that is what I mean. You are stressing on this for no reason. Do you plan on marrying me or what? Why the interrogation?” he said with an evil laugh.

"In your dreams!" I answered before hanging up.

I was proud of myself for getting him to admit to being involved with the website and luring him into naming Monica and Aaron as accomplices as well. I smiled with satisfaction and hoped that the FBI captured the whole conversation on record.

CHAPTER SEVEN

The Other Girl

I arrived at the terminal at LAX, thanked the Uber driver, grabbed my one carry-on bag and made my way into the terminal. I swiped the e-ticket on my phone at the self-check-in kiosk and hurriedly went through the security checkpoint without incident. I ran to the gate to catch my flight which was just starting the pre-boarding process. I stopped long enough to catch my breath and fetch my cell phone from my purse. I dialed Sam's number. It rang and rang before going to voicemail. I left a message, "Hey babe, I'm at the airport. I'm calling to check in before I get on this non-stop cross-country flight. I hope you are okay. Please call or text me ASAP to let me know you are okay. My plane lands in New York at 9:15 PM. I need to know that you are alright. Call me." I then texted him an abbreviated version of the voice message.

I paced back and forth at the gate, checking my phone every few seconds to see if he had responded. I finally boarded the plane and took my seat in first class. I clutched my phone in my hands, staring at the screen, praying for a response from him before the flight attendant demanded that all electronic devices be turned off. All I could think about was Sam lying on the floor bleeding to death - or being arrested for murder. I wasn't sure in my mind, which scenario would be worse. To ease my mind, I popped a couple of pills and got a couple of shots of vodka from the flight attendant once we took off. It was the only way that I could calm my nerves for the whole four-hour flight. I took a few deep breaths as the cocktails coalesced with the pharmaceuticals in my system.

During my first year at college, I had met Sam on an online dating website/chatting app. Our relationship started out platonic, but quickly escalated to a fuck buddy status when I made several trips to visit him at the campus and even paid for him to fly out to California to visit me. I admit that I was kind of a bitch to other people (especially girls) on the app, but I was nice to him and the sex was great.

I think I took pleasure in destroying the other girls on the app because of the torment that I endured in high school from bitches like them. This was my outlet for revenge and my means of eliminating female competition from my life. Let's face it, I was no beauty queen back in my high school days. I was a late bloomer and struggled with weight early in my life. The girls in school were mean to me, calling me names and body shaming me because of my physical appearance. There was nothing I could do about the fact that I was fat and had no control over it. I never ate a lot, but had some issues with hormonal balance. Luckily, I am the daughter of a rich businessman and could afford the best doctors, health coaches and personal trainers. Over next few years, I was able to get in perfect shape and develop into what most guys would consider very sexy; however, my high school experiences made a lasting impression on how I viewed and treated other women. I'm still insecure because of it and feel that every woman is trying to compete with me on looks.

One day I was very upset and called up Sam to ask for his help.

"What can I do for you?" he asked, eager to help.

"I want you to fuck a girl for me," I said rather matter-of-factly.

He was shocked by my request, so he asked, "But why would you want me to do that?"

"I want you to fuck her and record it on webcam."

"You're crazy! Why in the world would you want me to do that?"

"I want you to record her on cam so that I can prove she ain't no good! I will pay for your time."

I'm sure it was the strangest request that anyone had ever asked of him, so he clarified, "Wait. You want me to fuck her on cam? How does that even work? Will I be on cam?"

My reply was swift and premeditated, "No, don't you worry about that. We will take you off and edit the cam recording."

"This is absurd! You wanna pay me for this?"

"I will pay you a grand."

"Wow. That's a lot of money - especially for someone you just met."

"Just do as I say," I answered with sternness.

"Um, okay. What is her nickname on the app?"

"I will text it to you. Stand by."

I texted him instantly, which demonstrated the urgency of the matter. He began his mission to get this girl to cyber on cam. It took a few days for his charm to finally work on her. Meanwhile, Sam and I did a couple of cam sex sessions ourselves. I considered recording Sam as well so that I could have something as collateral, in case I ever needed it in the future. I also realized that he could outsmart me and do the same, or maybe even use something different altogether that he may have on me.

In about a month's time, he recorded the girl who was bothering me. As promised, he delivered the cam recording to me, which I used to blackmail that poor girl. It was mere amusement for me - and a thousand-dollar payday for him.

I know he considered the possibility of making lots of money doing this. He tried to stay close to me and observe who I disliked online so that he could suggest that we do the same thing and eventually get all of my female rivals on cam. He invested part of his thousand dollar earnings into buying apps and learning about new bots and software.

His plan was rolling along nicely until I called him and said, “We need to talk.”

“What happened? Is someone bothering you again?” he asked.

“My dad checked my bank statements. I can't give you any more money. The fun is over now.”

Of course he was disappointed, but he played it off, “Oh, that's fine. We will figure out something.”

“I am out,” I affirmed.

He didn't want to show that he was weak. Honestly, he must have been anticipating that this would happen, as he knew the gravy train would probably end one day anyway. He figured I would run out of money or lose interest in bad-girl games.

He had his own plan so he suggested, “How about we set up a website?”

“How would you make money out of a website?” I inquired with interest.

“We can sell ad spaces. Porn sites are gold for advertisers.”

“Who would want to advertise on such content?”

“I don’t know, but I bet they’re out there and I’m willing to find them. What do you say?”

“Whatever,” I said as I dismissed his idea.

“So, are you in or out of the fun game?” he asked to bait me. He knew I couldn’t resist.

“I am completely in for the game, but I don’t want any money flowing into my account. My dad would freak out and start asking lots of questions.”

He thought for a moment and then said, “I’m glad I don't have a dad. This works even better for me.”

“You don't mean that, do you?”

“Which part of it?”

“The part about not having a dad to worry about you. That part.”

“I totally mean it - I don't have a dad to worry about me, nor do I want one or need one!” he affirmed.

His website idea turned out to be a good one and the new business venture started to profit nicely. With his newfound wealth, he decided to upgrade his lifestyle.

“Monica, I want to move out of this shit hole,” he said abruptly during one of our conversations about the website.

“Do it! What's stopping you?” I asked.

“I guess I just need a little push.”

"Aww baby, why don't you move to New York? I will help you find a nice apartment there."

His logic combined with his fear as he reasoned, "What will I do there? I still have two years in college."

"How much money have you got?"

I knew the site was doing very well, but I was shocked when he replied, "About a million."

"Are you earning the money because of your education? Or have you been able to make money with no help or education, whatsoever?"

He thought for a moment and agreed, "Yes, that's true."

"I will fly to New York this weekend, and I will meet you there. We will find you a nice place."

The same weekend, we both met up in New York and stayed at the Plaza. We had some fun at the royal suite before finding an apartment in Manhattan. He really upgraded his lifestyle right into a penthouse on the 18th floor of a very nice apartment building in Manhattan. We shopped around for some furniture and basic things so that he could survive for a month without me.

While decorating his place, he hit me with an idea out of the blue. "I think we should add someone to our team," he suggested.

"Why?" I asked.

"We need people to handle all the money and make the right kind of investments. By the way, I am planning to buy a gun as well."

"Do you have someone in mind already?"

"Yes, I do. I need your help to get him on board. Could you stay here for few months and help me figure everything out?"

"Sure! I will. Anything for you. But why the gun?"

"I don't know, I just feel like I might need some protection now that I have all of this money and nice stuff," he said as he led me into the bedroom and pointed to the bed. "Now take off your dress and let's break in this new bed!"

I immediately got turned on at the anticipation of what was about to come. l loved his nomadic lovemaking techniques and that he was not rough, but still a little crude in nature. I thought about teaching him ways to get better, but instead I decided to succumb to his ways.

I slowly swayed my body across his as I started to unzip the back of my dress in a sultry manner. I slid the dress off of one shoulder as I turned and then slipped my other shoulder out as well. The dress slid down over my breasts and stopped when it rested on my curvaceous waist, I then coaxed it past my hips as I slid my hands down my abdomen and into the soft fabric of the dress. With very little effort, I freed the dress from my waist and allowed gravity to slide it the rest of the way down my legs and onto the floor. I stepped one foot out of the crumpled dress and then the other foot followed. I was glad that I chose to wear one of my favorite and very expensive bras and panties. I slowly unclipped my bra and freed my breasts from their restraint. I then turned and bent over slightly as I slid my panties over my supple ass cheeks. I then made my way to the bed and invited him to join me with a beckon from my index finger.

I had previously learned that he didn't like for me to make any sounds during sex at all - no moans, no cries, no dirty talk, no nothing. Any sound I made resulted in him choking me with his hands or anything that he could get his hands on. I still remember the very first time it happened. I was moaning in pleasure when he started to choke me with his bare hands. Thinking that he was more aroused by my moans, I started to get louder. His grip on my neck got so tight that I let out a squeal. I struggled to escape from his hold and get air when he suddenly released my neck, but slapped me across the face. It brought tears to my eyes, but he got off on it.

"Think of me and play with yourself," he demanded as I flopped onto the new, crisp linens.

Sam wasn't the kind who worked on role play or foreplay; he would jump right on me when his dick was still flaccid. He wouldn't go for vanilla sex either, though - bondage and dominance was more of his style. He would not have me get on top and take the lead. He has a certain sadism about his demeanor. He would frequently pull out and just stand up straight, right when I am about to hit my peak. Then he would just stand there and do nothing at all while I begged him to finish me off. Instead, he would just stare through me while I longed for him to fuck me some more!

When he first pulled this stunt on me, I simply got dressed and walked right out on him. He didn't even utter a word, let alone try to stop me. Then, he didn't even call me for days. This made me feel even more insecure and undesirable. I always ended up caving in and calling him, just to check in and see whether he was still around or mad at me, but he never seemed to show any remorse or reaction to the situation. Feeling frustrated over the situation, I decided to handle it differently the next time. So whenever he acted out, I would simply go south on him and arouse him enough to get back inside of me and finish his job. He couldn't resist my soft, moist lips around him, sucking his dick like a lollipop. I would tease him and say, "What flavor is the lollipop today?"

These thoughts ran through my mind as I lay on his new bed in the new apartment. I closed my eyes and let my fingers begin rubbing my clit. I sensed him crawling into bed on top of me as I opened my eyes and flashed a seductive smile.

"You did good so far, now come here and let me do the rest," he said as he mounted me.

For some reason, it always felt like he needed to dominate me in a brutal fashion. I know he has the potential to act like a gentleman, but it always gives way to his dominant nature. He always reverts back to the nomadic village boy that he truly is. It's totally the opposite of my high society lifestyle, where every silver spoon and fork is perfectly polished - maybe even solid gold and studded with diamonds! Being with him makes me feel like I'm living life on the edge in this secret relationship we share away from the rest of the world. It's the perfect example of how opposites attract - the refined me and the raw him!

I spread my legs wide apart, inviting him in. My upper body arching up, as I raised my knees up to fully expose my pussy. He spit on his fingers and rubbed them on my clit, as he slowly leaned towards me. I held my own head with both hands, pulling my hair down to their roots. I arched my back some more, thrusting my body upward toward him.

"Fuck me!" I begged as he slid inside of me. I repeated myself over and over again, "Fuck me hard!"

I wrapped my legs around his waist and let him dig into my pussy deeper. He started out slow at first, but quickly picked up his pace as I got wetter and wetter. My juices were flowing and my crotch got slippery and soaked. He pumped me faster and harder, as his balls slapped against my butt cheeks. I bit into his shoulder as I began to enjoy it more.

"Oh my god... Oh my god… fuck," I shouted as my body turned into an inferno and our sweat turned into steam on my skin.

Then all of a sudden, he just stopped and pulled out. "Not now Sam! Not now! Fuck!" I begged of him.

He smiled and grabbed my ankles, and with a jerk, he pulled me to the edge of bed. He grabbed me by the shoulders as he re-entered my quivering flower. His hands moved from my shoulders, till they found a firm grip around my neck. His grip got tighter and tighter as he pumped me harder and harder. I could see his jaw clenching and his brow furrow as his ears turned red. I knew he was about to cum. He choked me even harder and I told myself to just hold on for a few more seconds and not choke to death before he cums.

I closed my eyes and gasped for breath until I finally felt him shoot his load inside of me. He rolled off of me as his splooge oozed out of my pussy. We both just lay there limp in post coital bliss as my breath finally returned to me and oxygen rushed into my lungs. In no time, he was snoring next to me on the bed. I rolled out of bed and headed to the restroom to drain the rest of his spunk from my box. I could feel a burning sensation on the skin around my neck. I looked in the mirror and saw choke marks. There were dark red finger prints all around my neck - holy smokes! I shook my head in disbelief.

As I surveyed the damage to my neck, he woke up and walked right into the bathroom to piss, completely ignoring the fact that I was right there. Then, without a word, he stepped into the shower to rinse off. I thought I would get in and join him, but he didn't move over. Instead, he asked me to bring him a towel, which I obediently did.

As I passed him the towel, he casually asked, "Monica, do you remember the guy I was talking about?"

I nodded in agreement.

"He is here in town, can you lure him in?"

I was pissed beyond belief. What the fuck is wrong with this guy. How the hell can he fuck me in that fashion and then just casually ask me to go fuck another guy. He clearly doesn't realize what he has or value me or my feelings in any way. It was clear that I was being too nice to him. He needs to learn his lesson and I was about to become his teacher.

I set my plan into motion and said, "Okay let's do it. I am all in. What's his name? Where can I find him?"

"I have it all planned out. I will deliver free tickets to a private event to his boss and I want you to be there and pick him up by the end of the night," he said as he towel dried after his quick shower.

"What happens after the night?"

"I will let you know. Let's see what he does," he said as he slapped my ass and then added, "You've been a good girl."

A few days later, I followed his orders and got all dressed up for this special event. He gave me a brief description of the guy and finally revealed that his name was Aaron and showed me his picture. He was actually kind of hot and I looked forward to meeting him.

It turned out that he was easy to spot at the party and I had no problem confirming his identity, since everyone was given a stick-on name tag when they entered the event. I gave him a drink and then rocked his world in a secluded room at the party. He gave me his address and phone number without hesitation. I hoped that he would call or text me later, but he didn't. My rule of thumb is usually if a guy doesn't text you the same night, it's probably not going to turn out well - or maybe he got another option that he liked better. So I hedged my bet and made my move, and just showed up at his place the next morning. It was a bold and risky move, but it proved to be fruitful.

My intention was to make Sam jealous by sharing a bed with the very target that he had turned me onto. I planned to take things way beyond the scope of what he had asked me to do. It was my hope that Sam would become jealous and bring me back to him swiftly and end this stupid game he was playing. Instead, I found myself shuffling between the two of them over the next few months. The drama took its toll on me and I felt as if my head was going to explode and my heart was going to break into a million pieces. I started to drink more and more. I became numb to sex and half the time, I didn't know who was inside of me or when I was getting fucked.

I hit my limit one day and barged right through Sam's front door. He was sitting on the bar stool rolling a joint. I grabbed the remote and turned off the TV which was blaring at full volume. I paced back and forth, panting and sweating with nervous energy as he continued to calmly roll the joint.

"Look Sam, I don't wanna go back to him. I want to stay with you. I belong with you."

I got close to him, placing my hands on his face, sobbing uncontrollably and begging him to say yes. The tears rolled out of my eyes and down my cheeks and my crotch simultaneously started dripping love juice as I caressed his face, neck and back. But he rejected my affection and pushed me away. My legs started trembling and I felt a sudden surge of stress.

"I beg you, please don't push me away," I pleaded. "Please listen to me. I will do what you want, but I don't want to go back to him. Please, please don't do this to me." I became exasperated and short of breath. I felt like I could pass out.

He got up from his chair, and stood in front of me, face to face. He bent his leg and raised his knee and nudged it into my crotch to coax my legs apart. He rested his forehead on mine as he slid his hand down my dress. With no foreplay or warning, he jammed his finger into my snatch. I had gone from wide open to lockdown mode due to my emotional roller coaster ride and my vagina definitely wasn't ready for the abrupt intrusion.

"Easy, that hurts!" I said.

His sadistic side took over and he jammed his finger in deeper as he whispered in my ear, "You are my bitch and you will be forever."

He picked me up and carried me on his shoulders towards his bed. He then dropped me like a bad habit right onto the bed and proceeded to tear my clothes off like a lion would tear flesh from his prey's bones. He jumped on me and thrust himself into me. After a quick pounding and another mild choking, he rolled off of me.

He looked me straight in the eye and said, "I don't think that you should come here anymore. Aaron might find out about us and that would foil my whole plan. Why don't you move in with him?"

"You have lost your mind. You bastard! How can you fuck me like that and then tell me to go move in with another guy?"

"You need to calm down," he said as he raised his finger authoritatively.

He walked toward the kitchen and lit up a joint. Then he walked back over to me, put his arms around my neck from behind and locked his arms as he raised the joint up to my lips. I shook my head in disapproval, but he forced my lips open and shoved the joint up to them.

"Take it in. Breathe. Stop moving!" he demanded.

I gave up and inhaled it slowly and immediately began coughing frantically. He laughed at my discomfort. Fuck him and his evil laugh.

He placed the joint in between my fingers and then walked away. As I inhaled more of his shitty weed, it became crystal clear in my mind that I should not be with him. Maybe I would be better off with Aaron. He might actually love me and treat me right.

The next day, I got all dolled up, packed my bags and headed over to Aaron's house. He gave me a very warm welcome and seemed genuinely happy to see me in spite of my unexpected visit. I told him that I would really like to stay with him for a bit, while I got a modeling gig going in town. I cozied up to him and moved into his place and spent the next few days trying to adjust to my abrupt lifestyle change. I was becoming quite fond of Aaron, but I couldn't erase the memories of Sam from my mind - both the good and the bad. I began smoking weed and drinking more frequently - neither of which Aaron approved of, so I began to hide it from him. Oftentimes, I would sneak away to Sam's house when I knew he wasn't home so that I could steal some weed or booze. Sam caught me in the act once and felt it necessary to dole out the proper punishment.

"Come here, bitch!" he said as he pulled off his belt and snapped the leather taught between his hands. I froze, stone cold, for fear that he was going to beat me, but he didn't. Instead, he grabbed me by the ankles and pulled me to the edge of bed and rolled me over. He pulled my panties down, spread my ass cheeks and then jammed his finger into my ass without any warning or spit for lubrication. It hurt immensely - he was all about hurting me; my mind, my soul, and my body. I laid there, biting into the pillow as he finger fucked my dry asshole as punishment.

I knew that I needed to get my shit together and break it off with both the men. I needed to go back to California, my home and my family.

I started dropping hints to both Sam and Aaron that I was no longer interested in either one of them. I would ignore both of them and simply sit on my phone and laptop when I was at Aaron's house and I avoided Sam altogether. I decided to try to turn Aaron against Sam to get my revenge, but my plan failed epically when Aaron ended up joining forces with Sam.

Aaron could sense that something was up with me. We hadn't had sex in days and I had snapped at him multiple times. I wanted him to be the one to initiate the conversation, which he finally did. He started the conversation off on a positive note and was conversational rather than confrontational. He said, "Babe, how are you doing today? How's work going? Anything new come up?"

With my phone clutched in my trembling hands, I said, "I think we need to talk."

I pretended to be nervous as I set the bait.

He gently started his inquisition. "Babe, are you on drugs or something? Have you been smoking or snorting something or popping pills? What's wrong, girl?"

I told him that I had joined an online chatting/dating community before meeting him and that I had become involved with a guy. I explained how this guy recorded me without my consent and put my personal information and videos up on a porn website. I shed some fake tears to make my story more believable as I continued to throw Sam under the bus.

"He is stalking me now. He forces me into drugs and sex," I whimpered as I wiped the crocodile tears from my eyes. "He made me sleep with other men too."

He pounded his fist on the table and then hugged me and promised to rectify the situation. I couldn't wait to see these two guys fight to death over me.

~

I quickly re-entered reality as the flight attendant woke me up and politely instructed me to return my seat to its upright position. I realized that I was sitting in a puddle from my alcohol and drug induced fantasy-filled sleep. Minutes later, the wheels touched the tarmac in LaGuardia and I made a mad dash to hail a taxi to his penthouse in Manhattan. I wondered if we would ever fuck again - or if he had been fucked for life.

CHAPTER EIGHT

Handsome Offer

I had been thinking through all the details and logistics of the auction for months. The success of this event was critical to me and the future of the gallery, so it was imperative that it went well. I considered several different scenarios, including an online E-bay style auction, a silent auction for private buying, and of course, a traditional live auction. Before coming to the conclusion to do a traditional live auction, I researched all the pros and cons of the available options. The live auction seemed to be the most logical method, but I didn't want this event to be 'traditional' in any sense of the word. Unique, exciting and competitive were the key aspects that I had been looking to incorporate into the event. I wanted the buyers to feel like they were part of something special, to ensure that they would come back to future events too and buy more art. Most live auction buyers were flamboyant personality types who loved the pomp and show! Why would I have taken that away from them? Instead, I planned to deliver just that, plus a lot more!

I grew to believe that a live auction would create more walk-in traffic to the gallery and therefore, we'd be able to sell a lot more than just the items on the auction list. I stared, for the very last time, at the inspiration board in my study room and I pinned the reserve rates of each auction item on the board with each corresponding piece. My eyes read through the list, memorizing all the numbers until I stopped on one large figure which kept me up all night. In the morning at the luncheon, I knew I would have to make sure that we had a buyer for this one particular painting.

The whole thought process was overwhelming to me. 'Deep breath, Tanya! Deep breath! One step at a time… one step at a time,' I told myself over and over again to calm my nerves.

I recalled what my father would say on certain important days of my life. He would always say, "I hope you showered today - and not with perfume, but a proper shower with water from the tap!" He knew me better than anyone and he was aware that I would frequently get so caught up in other priorities in my life that I would not make time to take care of myself. He made me laugh all the time. His jokes had deeper meaning and always brought me back to reality, causing me to focus more on myself. I love him and miss him so much! Every single day, at least once, I stop to think about him, hoping that he is proud of me. The same is true for my mother - I hope they are both proud of me.

As the event time drew closer, I could feel the excitement and anxiety building in my heart and soul. Unable to sit still or focus on anything else, I decided that it was better for me to be at the gallery with my staff rather than working from home. As I stood in the closet, perusing my wardrobe options, I defaulted to my favorite blue dress with hot pink heels. I found myself debating on the hot pink belt for a ridiculous amount of time until

I finally decided to skip the belt today. I didn't want to look hip.

Thankfully, it was a quick drive to the gallery as the roads were clear. I arrived at the gallery at 6 A.M. and to my surprise, Mrs. Martha walked in shortly after me. She couldn't deal with the pressure or anxiety either, prompting her to come in early just like me. The catering company and the rental company arrived shortly after us as well. In a matter of an hour or so, the gallery was transformed into a fine dining venue.

There were some round tables at one half of the gallery with rented ghost chairs. The tables were adorned with some stunning flower arrangements to enhance the ambience. On the other side of the gallery, we lined up the paintings, sculptures and other artifacts on display. Any pieces that were above one million dollars were supposed to be displayed in a secure box or the insurance regulations allowed us to use a replica for display instead. Tonight, we had only one such painting that could potentially sell around that price point. After careful thought, I decided to put it in a box rather than use a replica. I felt that a replica could lower the chances of getting a higher price for this unique painting.

Everyone bustled about the gallery with haste. It was nice to see everyone from the furniture rental people to the caterers, the security guards and the auction staff working in unison as a team. All of my pre-planning and vendor choices were coming to fruition nicely. As each piece of the puzzle fell into place, my anxiety eased a little bit more.

Noon crept up on us and before we knew it, we had our first buyer walk into the gallery from the hotel. I stayed behind the scenes and let Mrs. Martha and some of my temporary workers greet them and show them around the gallery. I didn't want to seem overzealous or desperate, so I let the staff do most of the greeting and entertaining while I met with the auctioneer to go over the list and reserves one final time.

Mrs. Martha stepped into my office and updated me. "I think it is time for you to make an appearance. About 80% of the buyers have arrived and they are eagerly waiting for your presence," she said with a nervous smile.

I finished up my last-minute work and then spent a moment to quiet my anxiety. 'Deep breath! Deep breath! One step at a time. One buyer at a time. One auction item at a time,' I reminded myself as I closed my office door and made my way into the gallery.

I held my head high and strolled into the gallery to make my grand entrance. As I walked in, all heads turned towards me and everyone's eyes focused on me. My job as the hostess was to study all of the buyers' interests and to escort them to the pieces of art that I felt would be appealing to them. I would talk up the particular piece of art and see if it matched their interest and budget. If I felt that it wasn't in their budget or didn't appeal to them, I would promptly introduce them to something else or move on to another buyer who had more interest in that piece.

Mrs. Martha helped me prioritize the guests and she would also make sure that I didn't get stuck with one buyer for more than five to ten minutes. While I was efficiently doing my job, I noticed a young man looking at the boxed painting. I doubted if he would buy it, but I continued to watch him out of curiosity. He was extremely handsome, I decided I would wait to talk to him last and find out what was really appealing to him.

Mrs. Martha came over and rescued me from an extended conversation with a buyer. She politely announced to me loud enough for the buyer to hear, "Miss Tanya, it's getting close to the time for your speech and then we will start the luncheon right after that."

"How much time do I have?" I asked as I excused myself from the buyer.

"About ten minutes," she whispered to me.

"Okay, let me catch up with one last buyer," I answered with a wink.

"Make it quick, Miss Tanya," she said, nervously walking towards the DJ to inform him to get the microphone ready.

I walked over to the painting in the box, hoping to catch the handsome young man who had been eyeing it just moments prior. He wasn't there, so I started to survey the crowd to find him. Luckily, I didn't have to look long as he suddenly appeared next to me.

"Hello," he said.

"Oh! You spooked me," I said as I blushed, trying to not let him know that I had been looking for him.

"I am sorry. I didn't mean to startle you. I am Nick Baker," he said as he extended his arm and offered a handshake.

"Hello, I'm Tanya, the hostess of this event," I said with a smile. "So, do you see anything that you like so far? I noticed that you were reading about this painting."

"Yes, I do see something that I like," he said as he flashed me a friendly smile, "but please tell me more about this painting. I can't help but notice that this is the only auction item in a box and I am curious to know why."

"Great question," I answered as I reciprocated his flattery with another smile. "This is the most expensive item at the auction. We have a policy to secure an item in a display box if it's bid price may near a million dollars."

"What is so special about this painting to warrant such a high price?"

"Well, this is a 1600's era painting by a not-so-popular French artist named Lafelle, but this particular painting has been retouched by a modern-day artist using expensive metals such as gold, silver, platinum and diamond dust," I explained as I pointed out the brilliance of the metallic flair.

"So, any paintings which contain such metals are considered valuable keepsakes?"

"Well, have you heard of Picasso? Les Demoiselles d'Avignon was painted in 1907 and is the most famous example of cubism painting. In that painting, Picasso abandoned all known forms and representations of traditional art. He used geometric forms to distort a female's body in an innovative way, which challenged the expectation that paintings offer idealized representations of female beauty. It also shows the influence of African art on Picasso. That painting was a large work and took him nine months to complete. The process involved him creating hundreds of sketches and studies to prepare for the final work. You know what? It is said that he also used human excreta in one of his paintings, but I'm not sure if that is gossip or a proven fact. I read it over the internet."

"Hmmm... Wow!" he exclaimed, pretending to be fascinated by my explanation.

"So, does this painting still interest you? Or did another item lure you to the auction?"

"I am into business and investments. This is a newfound interest and I am still exploring my options. I do like the painting, but I really want to know what you like about it. It seems very unusual."

"Great question. I am half French, so there's that. Plus, my mom was a painter and she was greatly inspired by this artist. This is one of his last paintings and it was recently sold at an auction for just a couple of thousand bucks. I didn't know what at the time, but I envisioned that something could be done to make this old painting worth so much more. It's extra special to me because my mom was so inspired by this particular artist, that she became one herself! Later, I happened to meet a modern-day artist who bought old, inexpensive paintings and turned them into revitalized, million dollar artworks by adding diamond dust to them." I leaned over and touched the glass on the display case as I admired the work. "I would love to see it sell at a great price," I said with confidence.

"Wow. That's an innovative idea, but it must also be a great risk, tampering with an original work of art that's over 400 years old. Some buyers or other artists may not like the idea of it."

"You are very right about that, it's certainly not for everyone, but business is all about risk taking, isn't it? You are in business and investments, correct? I would consider this a calculated risk. It's the uniqueness and the risk factor that makes it so valuable at the end of the day." I gave him a warm smile and he nodded in agreement. "I hope you enjoy the event and your time in our city," I said as I smiled and excused myself.

Mrs. Martha marched towards me and placed her hand on my back, lightly pushing me towards the middle of the gallery. The DJ quickly pinned the wireless mic on me while I glanced back over my shoulder to get another peek at Nick, who happened to be looking in my direction. I waved at him and mouthed, "I will catch you soon," to him from across the room. He smiled, acknowledging my comment.

Mrs. Martha handed me a printed copy of my speech and wished me luck.

The DJ brought the crowd to attention as the roar of dozens of conversations diminished into silence. Once the buyers and media had taken their seats, the DJ then looked me in the eye, introduced me and asked everyone to give a round of applause. The feeling of being the center of attention and the lady of the hour took me back to my first recital - I remember being all dolled up and ready to perform for the first time as a child. I took a deep breath and started my speech.

"I would like to thank you all for coming to the first ever Auction Retreat at our Art Gallery. We have had the pleasure of working with most of you for the last three decades. It's an honor that we are able to continuously add new members to our auctions and grow.

First things first, I am both nervous and excited; as most of you know, this is my first event, so please excuse me if I come across like a child who just discovered Santa Claus.

I thought a lot about tonight and what I should share about myself that is relevant to this auction night. As I looked through years of my father's achievements, it occurred to me that this is not about this one night. In all of his years, my father didn't just execute the best auction nights with state of the art artifacts, but he made memories which he cherished. My father was a trustworthy dealer, an honest businessman and a loyal friend who was there for you. He was loved by all!

I, Tanya Simpson, daughter of Jeff Simpson, would like to assure you all that I will follow his path of being loyal, trustworthy, compassionate, and respectful, but most of all, I will cherish each moment with all of you tonight and forever."

The crowd got up on their feet and started to applaud loudly and passionately for the longest time. It was my first speech and it came with a standing ovation! The DJ actually had to step in and play the background music to quiet the room. He asked all guests to be seated so that lunch could be served. It took about another thirty minutes for them to finally settle down and start eating. I walked towards the DJ so that he could take off my wireless mic, but I was told to keep it on longer.

A reporter from the daily newspaper jumped up and took over the DJ's microphone. She introduced herself to the crowd and requested that the floor be open for questions. She said that some of the reporters would like to know more about me. Mrs. Martha walked me to my table and I sat down, still mic'd up. All of the reporters and news channel personnel were seated at the same table right across from me.

"Miss Tanya," one of the reporters asked as they took the microphone, "What are some of your favorite accomplishments?"

I addressed the reporter with a smile and answered, "Well, let's start with tonight. Tonight's a night that I am very proud of. Considering my background in business management, I'm really excited about the new buyer's retreat program that we have introduced, and that our team has been working on for months. This program will help buyers and vendors save time and money - and make the auction process fun!"

Another reporter asked me what motivated me.

"My family, friends and the people that I have the pleasure of working with. I believe in God, myself and others around me and I appreciate what they have to offer to make this world a better place. I am always on a quest to try new things, learn more skills and travel around the world."

"What's your biggest challenge?" asked another reporter.

"To stay content with what I have achieved as a person and as a young entrepreneur. I feel success is just never enough - and that keeps me awake at night a lot!"

The microphone made its way around the reporters' table as the guests ate their lunch and listened to my thoughtful answers.

"What is my guiding philosophy?" I repeated the question asked by another reporter who didn't speak into the mic clearly. "Well, there is a phrase often repeated by my parents, 'Do your best and forget the rest'.' I try to do my best as a daughter, friend, responsible citizen and a human."

"We would like to know a fun fact about you!" asked another TV reporter who hijacked the microphone.

"Hmmm… fun fact… well, I have never had a cup of coffee or tea." I didn't know how fun that fact was, but my answer certainly got a laugh out of the crowd.

"What advice can you give to others?"

"Be available, for a great opportunity only knocks once. Be persistent and aim for long-term returns."

Many more questions followed, but we had to wrap it up as we didn't want it to be all about me. After lunch was finished, we closed the gallery for a few hours so that we could transform it into an auction site.

We had the moderator and auctioneer checked in, the security guards in place, the theatre style seating set up, and the rest of the details were ready to go as well. It took about four hours for all of that to happen. When we finally had the auction items lined up, the buyers started to arrive and filter into the room, taking their designated seats.

The auctioneer wasted no time getting the action started. He started the event off with a sculpture. The opening bid was $35,000 and it ended up selling for $75,000. Things were really rolling and the next few items also doubled or tripled our minimum reserve. The auctioneer really knew how to incite excitement from the crowd. I couldn't believe how fast he could talk. It was almost like he was speaking a foreign language!

After each painting and artifact reached its max and was awarded to the highest bidder, Mrs. Martha and I got busy crunching numbers to calculate the sales commission, the secured shipping cost and the IRS sales tax - to curb our anxiety about the profit margins. Things were adding up quite nicely - and then the spotlight turned to the 'risk taker painting' in the display box.

The auctioneer slowed down the cadence in his voice and made a more dramatic introduction that was appropriate for a painting of its worth. "Last, but certainly not least, let me introduce you to a modern experimentation. This is an original 1600's painting by a French artist named Lafelle that has been retouched with precious metals and stones by a modern-day artist. Please refer to your catalogue for further details. The bidding starts at $250,000."

The auctioneer had strategized with me earlier and we decided to start the bidding on this special painting well below the reserve minimum in an attempt to build excitement while not scaring anyone away with such a high price to start. I held my breath in nervous anticipation to see if the strategy would work. Buyer 22 took the $250,000 bid and then was quickly trumped by buyer 14 who bid $270,000. After that it went to 320,000, and then up in increments of $50,000 until it stopped at $470,000. I held my breath as the auctioneer rattled off "$470,000 going once… $470,000 going twice… it was the longest bid ever. I was on the edge of my seat. We still hadn't reached my minimum reserve yet.

Then, just as the auctioneer was about to drop the gavel and award the bid on the third call, a deep, manly voice echoed from the back of the room, "One million dollars!"

The room roared with shock as everyone turned to see who had just trumped the bid from $470,000 all the way to one million dollars. My heart fluttered when I confirmed that the voice belonged to Nick Baker. That handsome young man made a handsome offer for my prized painting. It took the auctioneer, the moderator and the DJ several minutes to calm the room down after such an astounding bid. It took me a lot longer to calm my heart palpitations.

"We have a bid for 1 million dollars," the auctioneer announced, trying not to sound too shocked himself. "Can I get a million one?... Anyone for more than 1 million dollars?... Last call and final bid for this amazing work of classic art meets modern art," the auctioneer announced.

When it was absolutely clear that no one in the room was going to even come close to outbidding the million-dollar bid, the auctioneer began his three-count call. "One million dollars going once… One million dollars going twice…" My heart pounded and my spirit soared. "One million dollars going three times… and SOLD to the gentleman in the back, number 77."

I jumped right out of the chair and rushed back to Nick and hugged him. He received my grateful hug with a smile, but didn't make any additional fanfare about the purchase. It seemed perfectly normal for him to spend a million bucks on a painting! I made sure he was going to the after party before excusing myself to tend to the wrap-up chores. Mrs. Martha and the temporary staff quickly and efficiently broke down the setup from the event and had the gallery cleaned in no time. The security guards placed all of the auction items into the vault for safekeeping until they could be packaged and processed for secure shipping or customer pickup. I busied myself in the office crunching all of the final numbers. When I calculated the final profit figure, I had to double and triple check it. The figure made me smile from ear to ear! Then Dorothy called me at the perfect time.

"Mama Sita, how did it go?"

"It went very well - actually very, very well! Are you coming to the after party?"

"Yes, of course. I am heading there now and I have a new dress for you too!"

"Awww, you didn't have to do that, but thank you! I will see you soon. Do you have the address for the hotel? I have a suite under my name, take the keys and I will meet you there."

I left the gallery in a hurry after I made sure that the security officers had put all of the items back in the vault. I double and triple checked the lock on the vault to make sure it was secure and that all of the cameras were running. I made a quick call to the secured shipping company and gave them all of the buyers' shipping details and made arrangements for pickup the next day. Then I breezed out of the gallery, literally levitating as I walked from the high that I was on!

I met Dorothy in the hotel room and gave her a great big hug before asking, "Where is the dress?"

"Here, open the zipper," she said with excitement as she pulled out a big bag from the closet.

"What is this? How much did you spend? Did you buy me a wedding dress? Why is it zipped up and all?"

"Don't ask questions. Just open it. You deserve this. You have no idea, you are such an inspiration to all of us," Dorothy said as tears of joy formed in her eyes.

I am thankful to the Almighty that I have such supportive and caring friends. I hugged her and got all emotional for few seconds. She rolled her eyes and pointed towards the bag, urging me to open it and put the dress on. She was so excited for the dress reveal. Steadily and slowly, I unzipped the bag as each inch of zipper revealed a gorgeous white French lace dress emerging out of it. I squealed a cry, "Oh my god! Is it the same dress? It looks exactly like her dress! Is it the same designer?"

Dorothy really outdid herself on this gift. She had managed to swipe one of my mom's old dresses that I had been keeping in my closet since her passing. She had the dress re-sized to fit me and then adorned with some precious jewels and glitter. I had always fantasized about wearing that dress, but it never fit me right. Dorothy explained that she had found a modern-day dress artist who suggested doing the exact same thing with the dress that my artist did with the million-dollar painting that was just sold. How thoughtful and ironic!

"It's just beautiful!" I shrieked with joy as I started to jump around the room in excitement. "THANK YOU. THANK YOU SO MUCH!... I love you Dorothy."

"Are you gonna make me cry or what girl? I love you too," Dorothy sobbed as she hugged me some more.

"I am gonna leave you for now and see how things are going in the ballroom. You get dressed and I will meet you downstairs," Dorothy said as we broke our embrace.

I was still jumping around the room and I launched onto the plush hotel king size bed. "Get hold of yourself," she yelled as she breezed out of the room.

"Oh my Lord! Oh My Lord!" I said out loud as I put on the dress, feeling that it was smooth as silk as the lacy fabric engulfed me, sliding onto my body. This dress made me feel totally in love with myself. I donned my new dress like a newly crowned princess and swiftly left the room and sauntered towards the elevator. As the doors to the elevator opened, I stepped in and looked up to see an unexpected face. "Oh hey, Nick!" I stammered as I was shocked to have run into him at that moment. His gorgeous smile threw me off guard and sent me into a tizzy. Not only was he so darn handsome, but he literally just made me a millionaire in my own right!

"Why are you surprised?" Nick said, offering his hand as he pushed the door open button.

"I wasn't expecting to have the pleasure of bumping into you right now!" I answered as I blushed a bit.

"Did you forget that we all stay at this hotel and that we're all headed to the same party?" he asked with a laugh. "The rest we can blame on our destiny."

I stepped in and the elevator started to descend to the ballroom on the ground level.

"Why are you staring at me?" I asked with a shy sigh.

"That dress is really something!" he remarked with his mouth wide open. "And you are too!"

"Would you like to walk me in?" I asked as the elevator doors opened. "It would make perfect sense," I suggested as I offered my arm.

"Sure! My pleasure, my lady."

We strolled through the front lobby and into the ballroom, arm in arm. I greeted each one of the buyers that had made a purchase first. We had lots of entertainment arranged for the night and the band was already playing. The night would later turn into a 'dancing with the stars' night. I made my rounds through the buyers and guests as Nick headed to the bar to get us drinks.

I wasn't in the ballroom a minute before Dorothy came rushing over to me.

"Oh. M. Geee. Who was the guy you just walked in with? Have you two been dating? You didn't tell me about it."

“What are you talking about?” I asked, confused.

“That guy who walked in with you, he was at the party we both went to a few months ago.”

“Are you sure?”

“I guess. I don't know with 100% certainty though.” When she realized that she was being paranoid, she redirected the conversation, “Don't worry about it. I don't remember. Let’s dance!”

We danced a few songs as Nick joined us on the dance floor with drinks in hand. I was having the absolute best time of my life. I alternated my attention between the dance floor, Nick, Dorothy and all of the buyers and reporters that were present at the party. Just when I was thinking about leaving with Nick, he dropped the bomb on me that he had to go handle some unexpected business. He promised that he would make it up to me the next night.

“I just don’t understand how he could split like that. What could be so important?” I complained to Dorothy.

“Well, I don’t know, but don’t let it get you down. You’ve got dozens and dozens of friends and clients here. Go party!” Dorothy urged as she placed a kiss on my cheek.

And so I did, relishing every moment of the successful day.

Chapter Nine

Date Night

I smiled with pride and hoped that I had become the strong, independent woman who was living the life that my parents had dreamed of for me. My intentions were clear and my focus was on success, in spite of all personal dramas or distractions. Emotions had become subjective to me based on the person or situation at hand; oftentimes eluding perfect definition or explanation. I have had many discussions on morals and ethics with friends, early on and throughout my life.

What is success? Is success having abundant money in your bank account? Or is success defined by being famous or being popular? The general notion is that any person who is famous and has lots of money is successful. Does that mean that a teacher who has been able to shape the future of hundreds of young kids throughout his or her career is not a success story? Granted, teachers are paid paltry wages and most will never receive the praise or credit that they deserve, let alone become famous; however, what about the next doctor, actor or president who benefitted from their tutelage?

Then there is the mother who decided to stay home and raise her children and support her husband in achieving his goals - is she not a success story? Honestly, a person who is able to go to bed at night, knowing that they did the best that they could do and made the most out of their time that day and found gratitude and appreciation in their heart is a success, in my opinion.

During an interview with the daily newspaper, I was asked what the biggest challenge for me as a business owner was. Without hesitation I replied, “The biggest challenge for me is to stay content. Success is never enough.” One of my friends countered my statement with another question. They asked, “What is the difference between being good at your job and being successful?” Well, that's food for thought!

As I walked back into the gallery, I saw Mrs. Martha gathering the remaining catalogs and picking up other items and some trash left behind from the event. She seemed happy! It was nice to see her familiar smile return to her face. It was the same smile that she used to have daily while working with my dad, but it had been lost for the last couple months due to all the stress of handling the planning and logistics for the big auction. I’m so glad that we were able to pull off such a successful event on our own. It was the biggest event that we had held since my father’s passing. Before this success, I had doubted myself and my ability to pull off taking over the business and keeping the gallery operating up to the standard that my father had set. My concerns were now non-existent. The only tough thing for me to do now was to cut loose all of the temporary staff and security guards that had been hired for the event and the days leading up to it.

Mrs. Martha leaned over to me, gave me a hug and congratulated me, "You did great, Miss Tanya. Your father would be so proud of you."

I hugged her for the longest time, "Thank you so much for all that you do, Mrs. Martha. There's no way I could run this gallery or host an event like this without you."

I missed my dad badly. I closed my eyes and embraced Mrs. Martha as if she was my father. After all, she was a strong connection to him and the gallery's history. I didn't feel like letting her go and I hugged her accordingly. She understood and started to pat my back and brush my hair softly. This made me shed a few tears of mixed emotion - both joy and sorrow. I finally let go of her and looked straight into her eyes and we both exchanged big smiles.

I composed myself and made my way to my office to write a few checks for my temporary workers. It was tough to have to part ways with them. Each and every one of them had been amazing in their roles and the teamwork and attitude from everyone had been phenomenal, in spite of working long hours and late nights. We had all been eating off of the same plate, so to speak and had become a professional family over the last few days.

I summoned Mrs. Martha and asked her to gather up the staff for a quick farewell meeting and the disbursement of their checks.

The entire staff lined up outside of my office, with the head of security proudly claiming his spot at the front of the line. I shook hands with each and every one of them, patted them on the shoulder, and handed them their checks, but not before saying and a few words to each of them on how amazing the experience together had been.

After everyone had filed through the line and received their checks and personal thanks, I asked the group, “So how would you guys like to celebrate?”

“How about PIZZA?” the head of security suggested. Everyone unanimously concurred and then we all burst into laughter.

The pizza parlor next door made a fortune off of the order we placed! I was glad that they were open late, until 11 PM on weekdays. I was in such a great mood that I even considered hugging the chef at the pizza place too!

I was overcome with an amazing sense of achievement. I had never felt this way before. Historically, everything I had previously achieved was done under the direct supervision and guidance of my father. For the first time, I had done something on my own from inception to completion. I came to the realization that I could achieve great things with the help of my great staff and the gallery as my foundation and vehicle to success.

I began to wonder, ‘What if I bought a business of my own or started another venture by myself?’ If I could accomplish this level of success at the gallery, I was confident in my ability to do other things as well. Who knows - maybe there were things that I could do better than what I was doing now. In the case of the gallery, I wasn't given a choice. I was abruptly thrust into the family business when my father passed. I stepped up to the challenge out of compulsion, rather than passion and desire. How would I know what I was truly capable of unless I tried and failed at other things? Or what if I tried and actually succeeded? Ah, there I go again - one thought leads to another and now I am opening another business in my mind. I need to contain these random thoughts and focus on what I already have.

Earning my MBA degree certainly helped me build my confidence and present myself in the right way professionally; however, I wasn't very skilled and I didn't feel like I was the best at any one particular task. I guess I didn't consider myself to be good at something unless I was absolutely perfect at it. Over time, I've come to realize that I can't be perfect because too many factors in life are out of my control - like that time I tried to go fishing. I got myself all psyched up and finally put my anxiety to rest. I was ready to bait the worm on the hook and reel in a fish. And then it rained and the trip was cancelled. I resolved that neither my failures or my successes were completely mine.

As everyone was cleaning up from the pizza party and packing up to leave, my thoughts were interrupted by my ringing phone. It was Dorothy!

"Mama Sita! What are you doing tonight?" Dorothy said in a happy and bubbly tone.

"Nothing at all!" I said with a smile because of her Mama Sita reference.

"Let me make your life a little more interesting. I'm gonna pick you up tonight - and you better dress to impress! I am going to invite Nick. He has a thing for you - and you need to get laid! Like real bad!"

"No, don't invite him," I replied out of shyness in spite of the fact that the thought of being around him made me blush with nervous excitement.

"Do you like him? If not, can I have him?" Dorothy asked.

Gosh, she was direct and in my face.

"Yes, you can have him," I playfully responded in jest.

"In either case, he will be there. I will let him choose you over me. I know for a fact that he wants to be all over you though!" Dorothy giggled.

"Okay, I will see you tonight," I said before cutting off the conversation.

I walked through the gallery for one last time that day as the sun began its descent and the artificial light in the studio overpowered the natural light from the windows. I surveyed the vault and quickly scanned the CCTV footage as I perused the buyer list and the artifact list. My last bit of business was to give a call to the hotel and confirm that all of the guests were able to check out. I picked up my phone and dialed the front desk and was immediately transferred to the reservation department.

"Hello, Miss Tanya. How can I help you today?" asked the operator.

"I just wanted to see if all the guests were able to check out and all final payments were complete."

"Yes, I can absolutely help you with that. Can I please have the booking code for the room block?"

"Sure. It's TSAUCTION."

"Thank you for that information. Can I put you on a quick hold while I check the registry and accounting for pending payments?" There was a momentary silence before she popped back on briefly to say, "I believe there are some pending payments. Please hold for a few minutes while I check on them."

While I was on hold, I wondered whether Nick was still in town. What if he had left already? I was sure Dorothy would have called him by now. He didn't mention having any family in town, nor did he mention about extending his stay.

My wandering mind was interrupted as the operator came back on the line. "Miss Tanya, are you still on the call?"

"Yes, I am. Please continue."

She gave me a full accounting and explained that all of the guests had checked out - except for one. She mentioned that one of the guests was upgraded to a king suite based on his rewards points, so there was a refund for that amount due to the fact that he had chosen to handle his own expenses. Some of the other guests had ordered food and drinks which were not paid in full, so I gave her my credit card info and asked for a copy of the receipt to be emailed to me.

“So who is the guest who upgraded to the king suite?” I inquired.

“Let me check that for you.” I could hear her fingers clicking the keyboard on her computer as I waited in suspense. She quickly announced, “It’s Mr. Nick Baker.”

This was quite interesting and it invoked both excitement and curiosity within me. “When is he planning to checkout?” I asked.

“I am afraid I can't share that information with you. Company policy,” she answered.

“I completely understand. Thank you for your help,” I said as we concluded the call.

After hanging up, I saw a text on my phone. It was Dorothy! The text read, “Get ready girl. I’ll meet you at your place in an hour!”

I frantically stuffed my things into my bag and rushed out of the building. As I strolled swiftly across the parking lot toward my car, I heard two sets of footsteps behind me. I dismissed a momentary thought of paranoia that someone could be following me and replaced the thought with the fact that it was probably just a coincidence that someone else was walking to their car at the same time. I didn't want to look back, so I just increased my pace and unlocked my car with my key fob in hand.

Then I heard a man's voice yell, "Tanya!"

I turned around and through the dusk light, I could see that it was the FBI agents dressed as security guards. I placed my hand on my chest and gulped as my mouth and throat immediately went dry from nervousness.

I suppressed the nervousness in my voice as I greeted them. "Oh, hello. You guys spooked me."

"Sorry for spooking you, ma'am," the shorter agent said in an apologetic tone before the tall agent chimed in more seriously, "So we have good news. We are proceeding further with the case based on some new information. We just wanted to update you that there have been no arrests so far; however, we have been tipped off that there is a direct threat to you. Would you like to go under the witness protection program?"

His stern tone conveyed the gravity and urgency of the situation.

"I am afraid I can't do that. Is there any other alternative?"

"A shooting was recently reported in relation to the organized online crime ring. We would like to post two officers outside of your home and your work. Do you feel safe inside your home?" the tall agent asked.

"Well, I do have this creepy feeling that someone has an eye on me. Have you guys been following me?"

"No. It's not recommended. That's why we installed bugs and surveillance devices in your house. Plus, you already have everything covered at your workplace. Are you still using the CCTV video there?"

"No. Not at all of the entrances and windows - just some of them," I answered as I clicked through all of the camera locations in my head. I took a deep breath and said, "I think I would like to have a licensed gun in my possession for added protection. I have had some training and I have practiced shooting before."

The shorter agent replied, "Sure. We will get that done for you. You will have some paperwork to sign. We will reach back to you very soon. It's advised that you do not visit Stephanie at the police station, though. Just in case someone is following or watching you."

"Okay. I won't. My friend is waiting for me, so I've got to get going."

It was surprising to me that I was intimidated by the idea of someone following me, but less concerned with the fact that someone was potentially trying to kill me. I said goodbye to the agents and got into my car. I pondered the idea of someone ambushing me. I decided I would prefer a shootout. What was I even thinking? Since when did I become a killing machine? This is getting way out of hand. I made my way down the familiar roads to my house and I tried not to glance over my shoulder and look in the rearview mirror at every turn and intersection. I decided to let it go for now and just party and have fun to celebrate the success of the auction. I pulled into my driveway to see Dorothy standing at my front door.

She greeted me with a friendly interrogation, "Why are you so late? How much can you possibly work?"

"Nah, I wasn't working. I was having a chat with some cops."

"Did you get a ticket? Wow, congratulations - it would probably be your first one ever!" Dorothy said as she sassed me.

"No, it was just a warning."

"Darn! Anyway, what are you wearing?"

I really hadn't had a moment to think about what I was going to wear, so I simply shrugged my shoulders. She pointed to the bath tub and ordered me to shed my dress. I rushed into the bathroom and locked myself inside, before she had the chance to strip me. She laughed at the speed at which I raced towards the restroom, evading her hands. Meanwhile, she busied herself by taking inventory of my limited wardrobe. I wasn't big on maintaining a huge collection of clothes, shoes and accessories. Most of what I have is expensive and exclusive, but I don't have a very wide selection. I heard her shouting from the closet to the bathroom to ask me if I would like to wear black. Of course not, that's one color my father never wanted me to wear - and she knew that! I continued my shower and didn't dignify her ridiculous question with an answer.

When she didn't hear a response from me, she moved on to ask me if I would like to wear pink or navy. Now those were two of my favorite colors. I emerged from the bathroom, fresh and rejuvenated from my shower. I decided to go with the hot pink dress that she had spread out on the bed for me. I dropped the towel that was wrapped around my body and slid the dress over my head and down my body. I slipped on some matching pumps and then applied my makeup and straightened my hair with the flat iron.

“So, who is driving?” I shouted from the bathroom.

“Nick Baker,” Dorothy giggled in response.

“No, seriously,” I countered.

“I'm being serious. He's on his way here now and will be here shortly!”

“Why would you invite him here without asking me first?”

“So that he knows where to take you after the party! Don't worry, he will be gentle with you,” she teased. “Oh, hey, he just pulled up. You look great. Let's roll!” She said as she coaxed me out of the bathroom.

I did a final check in the mirror and took a deep breath to calm my nervousness. ‘You got this, girl!’ I thought to myself as I flashed a smile in the mirror.

We both rushed out the front door and walked briskly towards the white BMW 5-series parked in the driveway. He got out of the driver's seat and walked around to the passenger side of the car and opened both doors for us while maintaining direct eye contact with me the whole time. He was such a gentleman and he looked dapper in his black suit which was complimented by a tight, white V-neck t-shirt. I was quite nervous and I tried to avoid eye contact with him, but every time I glanced up, his bright blue eyes were staring into mine. In spite of his gentlemanly gestures, his entire demeanor was intimidating to a certain extent, but he had the cutest smile on earth! And those sparkling eyes and cute face... I knew I might develop a crush real soon. I slid into the back seat with Dorothy, leaving the front door open and the front passenger seat vacant. He closed our door and returned to the driver's seat. He glanced in the rearview mirror as he clicked the car into gear.

"Are you ladies ready to party?" he asked as he gave a slight wink in my direction.

I was speechless due to nervousness. I was already planning how I would respond if he asked me to dance at the club, and this simple question threw me off guard.

Dorothy chimed in to deflect the awkwardness of my silence. "I'm ready for some boots n cats!" she giggled.

"Huh?" Nick and I asked simultaneously.

"You know... boots n cats, n boots n cats, n boots n cats," she chanted as she mimicked the sound of techno music beats as she threw her hands up and thrust her body around wildly in the back seat as if she was already dancing at the club. It was the perfect icebreaker as we all had a good laugh.

We rolled up to the valet at the club and Nick escorted the two of us in, each of us arm in arm on either side of him. The lounge scene was impressive and posh. There was food and booze galore and the bass reverberated some 'boots n cats' music as bodies undulated on the dance floor. Nick dropped a few hundred dollar bills on the hostess and we soon had our own private booth and a few bottles of booze as well. Dorothy poured herself a drink and then headed to the dance floor where she quickly latched on to a guy who was dancing solo.

I sat there in the booth, blushing with nervousness, hoping that he would ask me for a dance. He scooted over closer to me, his shoulder touching mine for a brief moment. I cut my eyes down to look at my dress, avoiding engaging in eye contact for the moment. Then he offered his hand and asked me for a dance.

The moment I placed my tiny hand into his manly one, he pulled me to the dance floor and then proceeded to whirl us right to the middle in the midst of hundreds of people, with the music blaring all around us. The flashing lights interrupted the otherwise darkness of the room long enough to offer up brief glimpses of what others were doing around us. Just as I was getting into the groove with Nick and starting to unwind, Dorothy swoops in and threw a clam-jam my way as she hooked my arm and danced our way to the other end of the floor, leaving Nick solo. I looked back to see if he followed us, but he didn't.

"What the heck, Dorothy? I was getting into…" I started as she cut me off.

"Chill out, girl. You need to relax and unwind. You're dancing like Frankenstein out there. You need a couple of drinks, pronto!" she said as she nodded her head toward our table full of booze. "Plus, you need to make him pursue you. A little hard-to-get never hurt!"

I glanced back across the dance floor to find Nick. I was hoping that he didn't leave out of boredom. Dorothy poured a couple of shots, which we knocked back immediately as my eyes continued to scan the dance floor for Nick. Before the vodka shooter hit my stomach, Dorothy shoved another one in my face.

I finally spotted Nick at the bar across the lounge. He was standing next to a hot chick and I was pretty sure that they were talking. Before I could tell Dorothy, a couple of people who she claimed we knew from high school happened to walk by and Dorothy stopped them to chat. She was going on and on about so-and-so from you-know-where and whatnot, trying to pull me into the conversation, but I didn't care and I couldn't stop looking over at Nick. Dorothy finally abruptly pulled me into the conversation with a direct question about something that I didn't hear. I fumbled over my words and made up some nonsense response about the place being cool, but the music being too loud. One of the guys in the group leaned over and said something to me, but I didn't comprehend the words coming out of his mouth. I didn't care. All I could think about was Nick talking to some other woman. If this was Dorothy's pathetic attempt to make him pursue me, it was backfiring epically! I pretended to listen to the pointless banter as I planned my stealthy exit from the group. I wondered if I had the guts to stroll right across the dance floor and into the lounge bar and barge right in between Nick and the hottie and plant a huge kiss right on his lips.

I cut my eyes away from the group conversation and back into Nick's direction, but he and the hottie had vanished. I panicked and was about to dart away from the group, but I felt someone slide their hands around my waist from behind. Just like that, Nick emerged behind me and squeezed my waist tightly as he pulled himself close to me, leaning over to blow gently into my ear. "Let me make some drinks on the rocks and offer up a toast to Tanya for her successful auction event!" he said as he grabbed a bottle of Grey Goose and doled out drinks to me, Dorothy and our visitors.

The vodka shots began to liberate me from my shyness and I took this opportunity to speak up and add, "...and to Nick for his acquisition of some fine art!"

We all raised our glasses, toasted and then proceeded to party like rock stars all night. The drinks were flowing and I loosened up big time. Nick and I bumped and grinded on the dance floor for hours. I danced like I'd never danced before! Some other guy cut in and tried to seduce me away from Nick with some dance moves of his own. Nick didn't even bat an eye as this competitor proceeded to strut his best stuff right next to me. Nick was just so secure and sure of himself that jealousy wasn't his thing. He let this go on for a minute before he finally stepped around the guy and regained his hold on me as he pulled me close and away from the other dude.

I lost all track of time as I was mesmerized by the hypnotic trance music and the colorful lights that flashed in unison with the beat of the music. 'Boots n cats,' I thought as I laughed to myself. I was intoxicated with booze and maybe a little bit of lust for Nick as well, but my body was so exhausted. I didn't feel too lame, after all, it was after midnight. I couldn't eat or drink or dance anymore. Dorothy was completely stoned and still trying to keep up with the crowd's energetic moves. And then she reached out and grabbed another guy's butt. They promptly starting humping and undulating on the dance floor along with hundreds of other horny partygoers. She's insane, but I love her so much!

Suddenly, Nick grabbed my waist and pulled me close. He flashed a smile and the black lights in the club glowed on his pearly white teeth. He blinked his ocean blue eyes as he gently grabbed my head and turned it to bring me face to face with him. He pulled me closer towards him and I just let my entire body weight land on his chest. I had hoped that he didn't have a hairy chest, and I got my wish. I just couldn't stop thinking random things about him, his smell and his body.

The DJ announced last call and the last song of the night as he changed the tempo up and started to play 'Remember When' by Alan Jackson. Nick started to twirl around slowly with me in his arms. He had such a firm hold on me. I rested my forehead on his chin and embraced the moment. It didn't seem like he had any other intentions for the moment, either. Halfway into the song, I flung him around with all my might and I started to sob. My ambivert personality decided to make an appearance and all of my pent up emotions started flowing through my eyes in the form of tears. I wanted to cry it out. I wanted to cry out all of the sorrow of this life, my past life and the afterlife; so that there was nothing left to be sad about tomorrow.

He slowly moved his hand and began to caress my head, brushing my hair with his fingers. Suddenly, my knees gave out and I dropped to the floor, landing in a kneeling position in front of him. The next thing I knew, I was in the fetal position, howling like a four year old who wants a Christmas toy that is out of his parent's budget.

He swiftly picked me up and moved me to our booth - he literally picked me up and my feet barely touched the floor as he dragged me to safety. He sat me down in the booth and explained that Dorothy had already left, pointing to show me that her belongings were gone. I was a mess, so he scooped me up and took me out of the club. He beckoned for the valet to bring the car, and when it pulled up, he opened the door and gently placed me inside. Somehow I managed to keep my eyes open in spite of my drunkenness, fatigue and the burning sensation from the makeup which had run into my eyes from my crying episode.

I must have passed out because I woke up in a limo with two strange men sitting across from me.

"Wait. What? Why the hell are we in a limo? Whose limo is this? Why do we have two men with guns. Am I arrested? But cops don't have limos to drive them around."

I startled myself when we hit a bump and I awoke from a momentary dream. I looked up and saw that I was sleeping in Nick's arms. I quickly cuddled up and hid inside of his jacket. I am that pigeon who shuts her eyes when it sees a cat, thinking the cat will not chew its head off. I was just praying that this was all a dream and that it would soon be over. I would wake up in my own bed. With the comfort of his chest and the safety of these thoughts in my mind, I relented to sleep and passed out once again. I was in and out of consciousness for the remainder of the ride. I was half aware of what was going on around me, but I pretended to be oblivious. I just wanted to go to sleep and forget about my crying episode at the club and start a new day fresh tomorrow!

After the long ride, I could finally feel my bed under my body. It was so warm! I was still the pigeon who doesn't want to open its eyes and see the cat leave. I could feel my feet moving, struggling to free themselves from the pressure and burden of the comforter that was still tucked in too tightly at the foot of the bed. I managed to wiggle them out from under the comforter, but damn it was freaking cold! Now I needed my cozy socks. What the hell? I realized that I didn't have my clothes on. I was buck naked and my brains were banging against my skull. I felt as if my brains would explode and ooze out of my head, just like in a zombie movie.

My stomach groaned and my bladder felt like it was going to bust. I also had the taste of vomit in my mouth. I slowly rolled out of bed and made my way toward the bathroom. I conducted a concert with every possible bathroom sound that someone could make. My urine hit the porcelain with force as if a valve on a fire hydrant had been opened. I proceeded to fart loudly and then drop a vicious deuce, thanks to the alcohol induced tornado in my intestines. Once I had nothing left to give, I dragged myself from the bathroom to the kitchen for some water to quench my dry mouth.

"Aaaaa!!!" I screamed at the top of my lungs with all the air and muscle strength I could muster up.

Nick was standing there, half naked, in my kitchen! I couldn't believe my eyes. I had no idea he was still there. My eyes did a double-take and darted down to survey his shirtless chest. I also noticed that he wasn't wearing any shoes, socks or belt. I stood there, still as a stone, in shocked silence with a weird, puzzled expression on my face. He showed no reaction, he simply smiled back at me and my confusion.

"Do you want some water or some juice?" he asked as he placed some toasted bread on a plate of scrambled eggs. As I moved toward him, his smile disappeared.

"Why are you naked? I mean half naked?... I mean shirtless or whatever..." He sensed my nervous tone as he placed the food on the table and then poured me some juice.

I couldn't believe we had sex - and I didn't want to believe that. It must have happened though. I was completely wasted and I was all over him. I was thinking through how it would have happened, trying desperately to remember in spite of my drunken memory lapse. I must have unbuttoned his shirt before I took off all of my cloths. He must have enjoyed every bit of me.

My mind was running wild as I tried to piece together the rest of the night. He interrupted my thought process and asked a rather ambiguous question, “Do you know what you did last night?”

I nodded my head in dismay, “Yes, I know and I take full responsibility. I was all over you and it just happened. I hope I didn't bite or scratch you,” I said with slight shame and an apologetic tone. “I imagine that I must have dominated a lot. I am so sorry. I am not the kind of person who jumps in bed with just anybody. Not that you are nobody to me. You are somebody, but not the one. I mean... can we just not discuss this? Never mind, I want to know… how did it happen and did… Was I rough?”

He laughed momentarily, but then dropped the butter knife and got a more serious look on his face as he made his way around the kitchen counter to pick it up. I was certain that he didn’t want to look into my eyes and tell me that it was the most unfortunate experience he had ever had.

Instead, he said with a heavy tone, “We got here and you pulled me into the bedroom and started to kiss me. You told me how alone you have been. You touched all over me and down there and then pushed me onto the bed. You just rode me like a hurricane.”

I was so ashamed of my behavior that I turned fifty shades of red. He leaned towards me, but I couldn't look his way. This time I turned away.

"Look, do you want me to continue?"

"No. I have heard enough," I answered with shame as I looked up at him.

He then broke out of his serious demeanor and started smiling, which he then replaced with snickering, which was immediately followed up with all-out laughter. He laughed loudly and bent double, slapping his hands on his knees. I timidly smiled back and asked, "So does that mean nothing happened?"

"No, nothing happened," he replied, still laughing.

I ran towards him to chastise him, "Why are you laughing so hard? My whole house is going to collapse with your thunderous laughs."

"Ha! I should have captured that on video - your reaction was priceless!"

He pulled me closer and tightened his firm grip on my waist and my wrist. It seemed like this was his technique to keep me from running away.

"But why are you without a shirt?"

"Well, you did throw up on me in the car last night," he said.

Well, that *would* explain the vomit taste I had in my mouth, I thought. "Do you happen to have something that I could wear?" he added.

"Yes, I think I do. I have my dad's shirts. Would you like one?"

"Yes, if it fits me well."

"Okay, let's try it," I said as I led him into my guest bedroom and opened the closet.

I handed him a shirt, but he didn't try it on right away, rather he paraded around for a moment, twirling the shirt on his finger.

"Don't tease me. Put that shirt on," I commanded.

I paused to stare at him as he slid his arms into the shirt and then buttoned each button slowly. He gazed up at me and we locked eyes.

"Why didn't you do anything with me last night?" I asked.

The Uber driver honked his horn outside my front door as he hurriedly buttoned the last few remaining buttons. I walked him to the front door and tried to delay his departure with some inquisitive affection.

He silenced me with a kiss and said, "You are fun to be with, girl," as he kissed me on the cheek and walked out the door, turning long enough to add, "I didn't do anything inappropriate with you last night because I really want you to know what I can do to you when you are sober. Last night was not the right time."

"Well, thanks for not date raping me… I guess," I said as he ran and jumped into the Uber, leaving me standing half naked behind the partially opened door.

I closed the door behind me and leaned against it, imagining what would happen if he came back right now. I glanced over at the freshly cooked breakfast on the table that he had cooked for me. Just then I heard the doorbell, so I flung the door open with a smile.

"Good Morning, Miss Tanya," said the FBI agent who was dressed as a pest control worker. I was startled and disappointed and I quickly grabbed a jacket off of the hall tree to conceal myself. I saw the ZigZag exterminator van parked outside through the window.

"Oh! Good Morning," I said bashfully as I welcomed them into the house as I peered out of the door to see if Nick was still around.

"Miss Tanya, here is your gun for self-defense. Please sign the paperwork - here, here and, initial here," the shorter agent instructed as he pointed to the highlighted areas on a stack of papers that he placed on my counter. Meanwhile, the taller agent just strolled right into my place with some device in his hand. The shorter agent explained that he was just sweeping my place for bugs.

I quickly read over the paperwork before I put my signatures on it. He interrupted me and inquired, "Did you happen to tell anyone about what we are doing here?"

"No. I didn't specifically tell anyone. Why do you ask?" I said as I finished signing and placed my pen on the counter.

"Well, someone tipped off Cobra about our plans to tap his online activities," the taller agent said as he made a pass through the dining room with his device in hand.

"Does that mean we can't close the app?" I asked.

The shorter agent assured me, "No. It just means that it is going to be tough to find him. He is apparently on the run. You need to be extra careful. He might come for you."

"By the way, who was that guy who was here last night?" the tall agent asked as he passed by with the scanner again.

"Oh, he is fine. He's just one of my high-rolling buyers from the auction night. We went out for some drinks with a friend of mine and he escorted me home."

"What is his name?" the shorter agent asked as he pulled out a notepad from his overalls to jot down a note. "His name is Nick Baker," I answered with a smile.

CHAPTER TEN

Threat

I rolled over in bed and glanced at the gun lying prominently on my night stand. I reached for it, but grabbed my phone instead, which was right next to it. I opened up my Spotify app and did a quick search for a song. I clicked play and then closed my eyes as the music started to play…

> *Remember when... I was young and so were you… Time stood still… love was all we knew. You were the first, so was I. We made love and then you cried... remember when…*

My heart skipped a few beats and my spirit lifted as Alan Jackson's lyrics made me 'Remember When' I danced with Nick to the song the night before at the club. I cherished the moment and enjoyed re-living it in my memory as the song invoked the exact feelings I had felt (minus the drunkenness) as he held me close for the last song of the night. God, he was so dreamy! I hit repeat as the song began to wind down. When it started over fresh, I experienced the flood of emotions all over again. I think I found a new favorite song!

As the song began to play again for the fourth or the tenth time (I lost track), the music was interrupted by an incoming call. I instinctively went to swipe left on the phone screen to reject the incoming call and continue my musical bliss, but I was glad I opened my eyes soon enough to see that the number on the caller ID was Nick's!

I quickly sat up in bed, cleared my throat and answered the call, "Good morning Nick! How are you doing?"

"Hey! Good to hear your voice. I am doing great. How about you?"

"I'm fine. Thanks for asking. So, I bet you are probably eager to come and pick up your prized new art auction piece. Would you like to meet at the gallery today to take a delivery?"

"Sure. I will head that way in a couple of hours. See you soon!"

I rolled out of bed and decided to burn off some pent-up energy by going for a very quick run, after which I promptly hit the shower and put myself together for the day. I donned my favorite pink and navy blue dress and jumped in my car en-route to the gallery. I couldn't stop smiling as I checked my look in the rearview mirror at every stoplight. I really hoped that Nick would hang around for the day. It would be nice to spend some time together and get to know him better. It's not every day that a handsome man pops into your life, buys a million-dollar painting from you and then chooses not to take advantage of you when you pass out drunk! I would really love to spend more time with him and get to know him better. As I drove the familiar route to the gallery, I began talking to myself, rehearsing what I would say to him. I took a sip of water and glanced in the rearview mirror again to make sure there was nothing in my teeth. What *would* I say to him?…'It was nice spending time with you, let's do it again.' Nah, that's rubbish! 'Thanks for getting me home safe and making me breakfast.' Nope, that wasn't a good lead-off either. I didn't want to bring more attention to the fact that I passed out in a drunken stupor. Hmmm…'What's your story, Nick Baker?…'

I pulled up and did another quick mirror check and then got out of my car, fixing my dress and straightening it as I stood up. As I walked into the gallery, Mrs. Martha greeted me with a list of to-do items. I knew that I'd better get to work and finish everything before Nick arrived. I tied my hair up in a bun and took off my jacket. Bring it on, task list!

I checked my watch, it had already been three hours, so I took a break after I finished my last call. I put my legs on the desk and leaned back, resting my head on the executive chair.

I closed my eyes and began to daydream, humming the Alan Jackson song as Mrs. Martha walked in and announced, "Miss Tanya, someone is here to see you."

"Okay. Send them in," I said while still relaxing.

"Well, um, if you could..." Mrs. Martha said as she cleared her throat and cut her eyes down to my legs on the table.

“Oh! Oops… I completely forgot. I am so sorry. So sorry,” I said as I scrambled to quickly remove my legs from the desk, falling out of my chair as it swiveled abruptly on me as I had shifted my weight too quickly.

Timing is everything sometimes - and this time the timing was not in my favor as Nick walked into my office just in time to see me sprawled out on the floor, legs in the air!

“Hey there, let me help you get up,” he offered in a gentlemanly tone.

I almost died of embarrassment as he extended his hand toward me. “Thank you, but I am fine,” I said as I righted myself without his help. “Maybe we should play it safe and sit on the couch - this chair is tricky,” I suggested in an attempt to dispel my embarrassment.

Mrs. Martha chuckled and said, “I will let you two talk while I order some food. How does Chinese sound?” She jotted down our orders and then excused herself from my office, closing the door behind herself to give us some privacy.

“So... why did you *really* want me to come here?” Nick asked with a raised eyebrow.

“Well, your painting is… actually, I… I *really* just wanted to…” I fumbled for the right words for a moment before I composed myself and continued, “I wanted to apologize for my drunken behavior the other night. It’s not like me to get drunk like that. I… I’m still trying to piece together parts of the night. I mean… I had a great time and all, but I… I don't seem to remember very much. It's very out of character for me. I keep having these flashes, moments of clarity, if you will, about the night." I finished with a silly smile to lighten the mood.

He placed his hand on my knee as he slid closer to me on the couch. My pulse quickened with his touch. "Look…" he said, "You were great. You deserved to celebrate. You had a very successful event. It's okay to cut loose and unwind sometimes. Just let yourself go every once in a while. You deserve it!" His tone was reassuring and his voice was so alluring.

"Um… one question… were we in a limo at some point during the night? I thought you drove me home, but I remember waking up in a limo at some point. Briefly… but I'm certain… Nevermind, it must have just been an alcohol induced hallucination," I said as I cut my eyes down and blushed with embarrassment.

"No. You're absolutely right. We started out in my car, but we did a quick switch and took a limo home instead."

"Okay. Um, but why?"

"Well, I didn't want to embarrass you..." he hesitated, but I nodded my head as if to encourage him to continue. "I laid you down in the backseat of my car and shortly after I started driving, you threw up."

I winced and furrowed my brow with disgust over my actions, but he immediately consoled me.

"No, really, it was okay. The car needed detailing anyway," he said as he gently rubbed my knee. "I called a limo to pick us up while I cleaned you up a bit."

"Oh my God, I'm so sorry. That's not the impression I… I just... Um, I *never* get drunk and puke!" I said as I chalked it up as one of the most embarrassing moments of my life - along with falling out of the chair just moments ago.

"Really, it was no problem at all. It happens to the best of us," he said to quell my anxiety as he placed his fingers under my chin and gently raised my shamefully lowered head. He looked me in the eye and everything got much better all of a sudden. But then I had another flashback of clarity from the limo ride.

"Was there anyone else in the limo with us?"

"No, why do you ask?" he inquired with concern in his voice as he continued to stare into my eyes.

"Nevermind… I just thought I recalled two guys in the limo with us, but I'm sure it was just the alcohol and my imagination." I smiled and dismissed the thought as I lost myself in his gaze.

"So, what do you think about last night? Would you…" He stopped mid-sentence, smiled, slid slightly closer to me and leaned forward. I started to close my eyes in anticipation of an ensuing kiss.

And then came a knock on the door, followed my Mrs. Martha's voice, "Miss Tanya, lunch is here!"

Of course, timing! I would have skipped a month's worth of meals to avoid the interruption at such a crucial time. Darn Chinese food and their speedy delivery! Nick sat up straight and we both scooted away from each other a little bit as I invited Mrs. Martha into the office. The sweet smell of Nick's Ocean Blue cologne was immediately overpowered by the smell of Gong Bao chicken and Ma Po tofu. I wasn't even hungry anymore. My appetite had shifted to something else.

"I'll take it from here," I said as I winked at Mrs. Martha with my right eye, opposite of Nick's line of sight.

I took the bag of Chinese takeout from Mrs. Martha's hand and smiled. I opened the food and spread it out on the desk, buffet style.

"So when do you want to take your auction item?" I asked nonchalantly as I plated some piping hot food. "How would you like to take delivery? Would you like me to have it insured and shipped somewhere or shall I have the armored transport pick it up and take it to a bank safety deposit of your choice?"

"Actually… it's for *you*," he said as he cut his eyes up to mine as I handed him his plate.

"Wait. What? No!" I was flabbergasted.

"Yep," he said with a proud smile.

"Nick, this is outrageous! I cannot accept such a gift from you."

"Yes. Yes, you can. And you will!" he said as he placed his finger on my lips to silence me.

"I will keep it in the vault for you for now," I said as I gently grabbed his hand and lowered his finger from my lips.

He kissed me on the cheek and said, "Let's eat!"

We noshed on some Chinese food and shared a few laughs until our bellies were full. I cleaned up while Nick flipped through some art magazines on my desk.

"Hey, I've got an idea," he proposed. "Clear your schedule. Let's take a little drive down the coast. There's somewhere I want to take you."

My heart skipped a few beats and my body got all tingly from excitement. I enthusiastically agreed and asked, "Okay, where are we going?"

"Well, do you like surprises?"

"Of course! Who doesn't?"

"In that case, I'm not going to tell you," he said with a smile and a wink.

I sent a couple of quick emails and let Mrs. Martha know that I would be leaving for the remainder of the day. We sauntered out of the gallery, arm in arm, and jumped into his white BMW 5-series. He opened the sunroof and the windows, and we headed out of the city and down interstate 75. I tried multiple times to guess where he was taking me, but he wouldn't tell - or even give me the slightest hint. We played a plethora of different music, each of us alternating the selection of some our favorites and classic songs. We sang at the top of our lungs as the wind blew through our hair. I couldn't believe the day I was having! I wanted to cherish and remember each and every moment.

It wasn't until we got off the exit in St. Pete beach that I had a hunch where he might be taking me. My suspicion was confirmed as we pulled into the parking garage adjacent to the Salvador Dali museum.

"Oh. My. God!" I shrieked. "I've been wanting to come here!"

"You mean… you, the art gallery owner... you've never been here?" he asked with a surprised look on his face.

"Of course I've been here. I came when they opened back in 2011…"

"Oh," he said as his enthusiasm was momentarily dashed by my comment.

"I mean, it's been a while since I was here. I absolutely love this place and I've been wanting to come back to see the Frida Kahlo exhibit that is currently visiting on display right now! How did you…"

He cut me off and grabbed me by the hand as we skipped toward the 75-foot-tall glass entrance known as the 'Enigma'. We got our tickets and then ran up the spiral staircase to the exhibit floor like two kids on

Christmas morning. Since I had seen Dali's exhibit before, we started out with Frida. We donned our headphones for the narrated tour, but I added lots of commentary after the brief audio description of each piece ended. Nick was impressed, but not surprised at my knowledge and interest in Frida's work. Her life's story included an accident in which she was impaled, inflicting life-altering injuries. She also endured tumultuous relationships and adultery throughout her life. Whenever I thought I had a rough life, I knew that thinking of Frida's journey in life would bring me back to a place of gratitude and appreciation.

When we had finished the Frida exhibit and absorbed every bit of her essence and art, I excused myself and went to the restroom for a moment. I whipped out my mascara and emerged from the ladies room minutes later with a Frida-style monobrow. I thought Nick was going to die laughing. I would proudly rock this look for the rest of the day!

Dali was also one of my all-time favorite artists and, since I had seen his exhibit before, I gave Nick a comprehensive tour and explanation of each and every piece of art. I saved the best for last as we concluded our museum tour with a 3D virtual experience of Dali's classic painting 'Archaeological Reminiscence of Millet's Angelus'. We swiveled in our chairs and simultaneously experienced the work of art from a 360-degree angle. It was such an amazing thing to see Nick experience it for the first time!

We left the museum and walked through the botanical garden and then down to the beach where we took a stroll on the white, powdery gulf coast beach, hand in hand, just in time for an epic sunset. We stopped to rest a moment and he wrapped his arms around my waist and pulled me close. I looked up into his sky-blue eyes as his neck extended and his face leaned in toward mine. I closed my eyes and pursed my lips as I felt his lips touch mine. It was the most sensual kiss of my life. I felt as if my feet were no longer touching the ground as I levitated in ecstasy. The kiss only lasted for a minute or so, but I knew that the memory might last a lifetime. It was the perfect ending to a day that had been perfect… so far.

Our hour-long drive back to Tampa was uneventful, but our arrival back at the studio would prove to be the contrary. We pulled up outside of the studio and parked out front. The streetlights illuminated the street and sidewalks. I invited Nick into the studio while I checked to make sure everything was in order from the day.

"I sure hope Mrs. Martha is gone for the day," Nick said as we got out of the car and headed across the sidewalk to the door.

"Why's that?" I asked.

"Well, because she is a hard worker. And… because of this…" he said as he grabbed me by the arm and spun me around to face him. He pulled me close and laid a kiss on me as we stood under the street light.

"Nick," I quipped, "There are security cameras." I cut my eyes toward the front of the gallery.

“Cameras, huh? I’m not afraid of being on camera with you,” he laughed as he kissed me some more.

Just as I was about to close my eyes and prepare for another kiss, I noticed two men in suits get out of a parked car across the street and begin walking in our direction. I didn’t think much of it at first, until I saw both of them reach inside of their jackets and pull out guns. The men picked up their pace as they walked our way, cocking their guns and drawing them up to point in our direction.

I screamed, “Nick!” as he quickly turned. One of the men fired a shot in our direction while the other moved to our side, gun drawn, for a better vantage point. Nick’s reaction was swift as he pushed me to the ground behind a parked car and dove behind me to shield me. I instinctively reached into my purse and hastily fumbled through its contents, finding my FBI issued gun. I drew the gun, cocked it and fired two shots in the direction of the man who was trying to flank us. Spooked and surprised by the fact that I had a gun and knew how to shoot, they both quickly retreated across the street and into their car, speeding off with squealing tires. Before we had a moment to collect our thoughts, I heard the roar of a car engine as the car spun around in the street and headed back in our direction, rapidly gaining speed. The window came down and the passenger’s arm emerged from the window with gun in hand. Nick pushed me back down behind the car and shielded me as a flurry of bullets ricocheted off the cars in front of us and the buildings behind us. The car sped off down the street, hopefully for good this time.

"Are you alright?" Nick asked as he frantically surveyed my body and brushed my tousled hair from my face.

"Yes," I said as my ears rang and my heart pounded. "Quick, before they come back," I said as I fetched the keys to the studio from my purse.

The air still reeked of gunpowder and burning tires as we dashed inside the studio, locking the door behind ourselves. We made a mad dash for the safest place I knew - the vault. I quickly entered the combination to the vault door and then we both rushed inside, closing and locking the door behind us. I immediately dialed 911.

"911 operator, what's your emergency?"

"Two men just fired shots at us. Please send police immediately. We are at the art gallery near MaxWell shopping center on 43rd street."

"Are you safe now?" the operator asked.

"Yes, well maybe," I said as I tried to catch my breath. "We are hiding in the vault. Please come quickly. They may try to return."

"Stay on the line and stay where you are. I have officers in route. Do you have a description of the men?"

"Yes," I said as I had a momentary flashback to the limo ride home from the club. I was certain that I had seen these men before. In spite of my drunken stupor that night, I was certain it was them. Nick caressed my back as I gave my description to the operator. "They were both white males, probably in their late thirties to mid-forties, about 5'10" to 6' tall, wearing black suits and driving a newer black Cadillac, I think it was a CTS sedan." Nick nodded to concur.

I sat on the floor of the vault with the gun on my lap and the phone clutched in my hand as I remained on the line with the operator, listening to her as she relayed the whereabouts of the gallery to the responding officers. I turned and glanced up at Nick as he rubbed my back, trying to quieten my nerves and stop my trembling.

I muted the phone momentarily as I locked eyes with Nick. "Who were those men?" I asked sternly.

"I have no idea," Nick replied immediately with a slight tell-tale twitch of his left eye.

"Nick, are you *sure*?"

"Yes. Why would I lie?"

"They looked so familiar. Were they…" I was interrupted as the operator returned her attention to me and asked a couple more questions.

When I finished answering her questions, I again muted the phone. Before I could address Nick regarding the men, he diverted my line of questioning with his own. "Where did you get the gun?" he asked as his eyes cut down to my lap.

I realized that I could not reveal the source of the gun to him, so I replied, "I am a single woman and I own an art gallery full of millions of dollars of artifacts. Why wouldn't I own a gun?"

"Right. Well, where did you learn to shoot like that?"

"Practice," I answered.

"Thank God you…" he started as the operator announced that the police were outside of the gallery.

The operator informed us that the police had swept the front and rear of the building and had secured the location. She instructed us to exit the vault and proceed to the rear door to let the officers in. We stood up, and before leaving the vault, glanced over at Nick's painting sitting proudly and safely on the shelf.

"Maybe they were coming to steal your painting," Nick suggested.

"You mean *your* painting," I said correcting him.

We emerged from the vault and secured the door behind us. Nick went to the back door to let the police in and I opened up my office and turned the lights on. I could see blue lights flashing and lots of commotion out in the street in front of the gallery. I texted Stephanie to let her know what had happened as Nick recounted the details of the ordeal to the officers as they made their way to my office.

The officers questioned both of us simultaneously, our stories matching perfectly in every way. In the midst of the report filing, my phone dinged - it was Stephanie. Her text read, "I want you to come to the station immediately so that I can relocate you tonight in preparation for the witness protection assignment."

I discreetly texted back, "I'm fine. Shaken up, but fine. I am safe. The gun saved me."

She responded, "I will radio to the commanding officer on scene to arrange a police transport for you."

I glanced down to check my text as Nick continued talking to the officers.

"Miss," an officer said, "We see CCTV security cameras on the front of the building. Can you provide access to the footage?"

"Sure," I said as I broke my focus on my phone, placing it in my purse for the moment. "Great idea. Let me see…" I nudged the mouse on my desk, bringing the computer to life from its slumber. I logged in and opened the security app and clicked on the footage, optimizing it and bringing the front store camera into full-screen mode.

The two officers, Nick and I watched the scene unfold and I discreetly pulled my phone out and started to text Stephanie back.

"Who are you texting?" Nick asked in a slight whisper so as to not disturb the officers.

"Dorothy," I instinctively answered, giving no indication or further attention to my lie. I swiveled slightly and subtly in my chair to keep my phone's display from his line of sight. "Really. Ok now. Want to go home. Have gun and friend with me. Will talk plans tomorrow." I texted back quickly.

I really just wanted this situation to be done with. I was exhausted, but empowered in that I had effectively protected myself and Nick from an ambush by two armed men. I knew disappearing into the abyss of the witness protection program was the safest, and possibly the smartest thing I could do, but I wasn't ready to go. I was emboldened from the shootout and prepared to defend myself again, if necessary.

Moments later my phone dinged, "Not smart. I can't force you though. We have our eyes on you. Lay low. Be safe."

We wrapped up our affidavit and statement with the police as they watched and replayed the CCTV footage. Unfortunately, the two men never got close enough to come into the field of view of the cameras, which were pointed right at the front door and a small radius across the sidewalk to the street. I watched on the video, Nick pushing me down and huddling over me to shield me while I drew the gun from my purse. If I had waited a few seconds longer to shoot, the men might have come into the field of view. I pondered whether they were aware of the cameras and if that was why the second man swept wide to remain out of sight. It empowered me to see myself shoot fearlessly over the parked cars toward the men. Nick's initial bravery, fear and then compassion for me was evident as I watched the video. Seeing the incident replayed in slow motion, afforded me a different perspective on the incident that had taken place in a flash. It also erased all my fears that Nick had any connection to the men as well. The officers made copies of the footage as evidence and then wrapped up their reports.

"Ma'am," one officer directed toward me, "Here's the plan. There's a lot of media outside. We recommend that you don't engage with them. If you would be so kind as to give us the keys to the gallery, we need to stay and continue to investigate the crime scene. We will secure the property and leave an officer here on guard through the night. We can either drive you home or usher you to your cars. The BMW out front has a few bullet holes in it, so we are not sure…"

"We can take my car. It's parked out back," I interjected. "We can also avoid the media if we leave that way." I looked out of my office, through the gallery and out the front windows as I saw two officers rolling out yellow crime scene tape on the sidewalk, between the light post and the front of my store. There were also spotlights and reporters with microphones and news camera crews giving live reports from the scene.

"Good idea, ma'am. We will have two officers follow you home to ensure that no one is on your tail. Would you like for me to have them remain and watch your house as well?" the officer asked.

"That won't be necessary," I said with an appreciative smile. And with that, we slid out of the back door with two of the officers. Nick and I jumped into my car and I navigated through the back alleys and out onto a side street a few blocks away. Two unmarked police cars followed us as discreetly as they could until we arrived safely at my house. We nodded our heads and gave a thumbs up to the police as they slowly drove off when we entered my front door.

I dropped my purse on the coffee table and turned to embrace Nick. In an instant, my passion became aroused and the feeling eclipsed my lingering anxiety about the shooting. "It's alright now," he said as he gently rubbed my back and stroked my hair. I leaned my head back and closed my eyes as he followed my lead and began to kiss me. He still smelled so good. My knees went numb and I got goosebumps. Just as I was about to suggest that we move to the bedroom, my phone rang. I leaned over the coffee table and fetched my phone from my purse. It was Dorothy calling. I knew if I didn't answer the call, she would probably show up at my house, so I took the call.

"Oh my God, girlfriend. Are you okay?" she pleaded.

"Yes. We are fine. Home safe now."

"It's all over the news. The shooting in front of your gallery," she rambled on, "Wait. We? Who is with you?"

"Nick."

Hearing his name, Nick drew closer to me.

"Put him on the phone please," she demanded.

Instinctively, without thinking, I handed him my phone. I could hear Dorothy tell him, "You better take care of my girl - or I will make it my mission to… let's just say I'll shoot you myself if anything happens to her!"

As she continued to demand and implore that Nick protect me, it dawned on me that I had told Nick that I had been texting with Dorothy earlier. I bit my lip as I hoped that nothing would be revealed to the contrary.

"Yes, you know I will," Nick assured her as he cut his eyes up to me and smiled a warm and genuine smile.

"We will be fine. Give us some time. I won't leave her alone. I promise."

He hung up the phone, tossed it back into my purse and then proceeded to sweep me off my feet and carry me into the bedroom. "You need some stress relief," he said as he laid me on the bed. He removed his shirt and lorded over me at the foot of the bed. I sat up and ran my fingers over his smooth chest.

He gently pushed me onto my back as he slid my dress off, lifting me slightly to free it from between my back and the plush mattress. He slowly crawled on top of me, gently placing his weight on my body. As he looked into my eyes, he moved his fingertips across my forehead and brushed my hair away from my face. He kissed my neck as his fingers traced the side of my face, moving towards my lips. As his finger crossed my lips, I playfully bit it.

"Ouch!" he replied in jest and then whispered in my ear, "You are indeed a wild cat!"

I froze. Time froze. "What?" I said as I pushed him away from me.

He continued to kiss my neck without repeating himself. I started to move away from him, pulling myself up towards the headboard. "Stop. What did you just say?"

"Nothing," he said as he leaned back in to continue kissing me, this time placing his arms on either side of my head and neck as if to trap me. I arched my back and squirmed, giving him, at least in his mind, encouragement to subdue me more.

"Stop!" I demanded as my passion surrendered to fear and anxiety. I needed clarity and I needed to get out from under him.

He lifted his right hand and slammed it into the mattress, inches from my head. "Fuck - I just want you so Goddamn bad! How many more interruptions could we possibly have?" he said as he leaned onto me more.

I could not take any more. My romance with him had completely waned and given way to fear and disgust. I planted my heels into the mattress and thrust upwards and backwards and out from underneath him. My maneuver worked and left him hovering awkwardly over the edge of the mattress as I sat upright with my back against the headboard. I raised my finger and pointed it in his direction. "Are you Cobra?" I asked with the most gravitas that I could muster.

"What are you talking about?" he said with a puzzled look on his face.

"Sam, I know it's you. You called me Wildcat," I said as I sneered with anger. "You tricked me - you are Cobra!" I yelled as I pointed for him to get away from me.

"I have no idea what you are talking about," he said with a calm, straight face.

"Nick Baker… Sam, Sam Baker, Cobra. You know exactly what I'm talking about!" I screamed as I lunged toward him in rage. He caught me and stifled my flailing arms' attempt at an assault, flipping me back onto the bed and then straddling me.

My heart raced. I had no idea what to do. He had me securely pinned down on the bed with all of his weight on my arms. Before I could think or formulate a plan, I heard a loud bang from the front of the house and a split second later, men in SWAT team uniforms came swarming into my room.

"Hands up. Get on the fucking floor," they yelled as their drawn guns focused squarely on Nick.

"Please, just let me…" he begged as the officers quickly subdued him, pulling his arms behind his back and cuffing his wrists together tightly.

Another SWAT officer tossed me a towel from the bathroom to cover up with. Nick was dragged from the bedroom and in an instant, I found myself half naked, wrapped in a towel in front of three complete strangers who were the SWAT team agents.

"Hi, I'm officer Brooks," one of the men said as he removed his face shield and armored helmet. "We were given orders to interject. You are safe now."

Before I could question him, the two familiar FBI agents walked into the doorway to the bedroom. "Ma'am," said the short one, "Our wiretaps picked up the hot word 'Cobra' and we detected your distress and acted accordingly."

Before I could reply, my phone rang - it was Stephanie. "Hold tight sister, I'm on my way," she said. Our conversation was brief and the officers on site were demanding my attention.

I recounted the entire day to the agents as they took notes and recordings. Minutes later, Stephanie arrived, breaking professional protocol and embracing me. She explained to me that they had reason to believe that Nick had tampered with a couple of the surveillance devices in my apartment the night before, but that he hadn't found them all. She also said that he may have previously drugged me. I struggled to rationalize the motives and the alleged actions. 'Why?' I thought to myself. After all, he just bought a million-dollar painting from me. What was he trying to do? Rape me? How? I was willing to sleep with him anyway! None of it made any sense to me. My head was spinning with thoughts and anger as I tried to process my emotions. I excused myself as I told Stephanie that I needed to use the restroom. I left the bedroom and headed to the living room instead of the bathroom. I walked out of the front door and charged toward Nick, Sam, Cobra, whoever he was. I kicked at his shins and shouted, "You lied to me. Why? Why? Why would you do that?" I screamed as I gushed with emotions and tears.

Several officers subdued me and separated us, while the other officers hastily moved Nick toward the squad cars parked out front in the street. Stephanie rescued me from the grasp of the officers. She hugged me and pulled me back toward the house. I glared in Nick's direction as the officers opened the rear door of the patrol car and pushed his head down as they put him into the back seat of the car. When the door closed and the two officers parted, I could see Nick staring in my direction out of the window. I swear I saw a teardrop well up in his ice blue eye and then roll down his cheek. Other than the lone tear, he maintained a perfect poker face as the squad car pulled away from my house.

After a few hours, almost everyone left, except for Stephanie. I was just staring off into the distance in disbelief, my ears buzzing and my head hurting. I had this incredibly intense, banging headache. A few times I broke down crying, soaking myself in tears. The feeling of being touched by evil was bothering me to the core. With the house less crowded now, I told Stephanie that I really needed to take a shower. She concurred and told me that she would be outside waiting for me. I grabbed a change of clothes, headed into the bathroom and immediately stepped inside the shower. I replayed over and over in my head how I had gotten so close to someone so evil.

Stephanie was still waiting outside of the door for me to come out, while I was hoping that she would leave. I dreaded having another conversation with her, so I took the longest shower of my life. It didn't help very much. I still felt filthy, from the inside out.

"Tanya, you need to come out now," she finally demanded as she tapped on the door again.

"Yes," I acknowledged from inside the shower as I turned the water off and grabbed a towel. "So what is next?" I asked as I patted my hair dry.

"You will have to be under the witness protection program. You really have no choice at this point. Someone fired shots at you today and you had an alleged suspect in your apartment. We have no clue if it is Sam or Aaron right now," Stephanie said through the closed door.

I placed my brush on the sink. "What do you mean? I am telling you that he's Sam. Why is there any doubt?"

"Honestly, we don't think it's Sam. It's not likely. Sam has been playing hard to get for the last decade. He is not going to come out for you. We believe he is on the run or planning his escape."

"It doesn't make sense that he would surface and reveal himself, you're right. But what if he finally met someone who set his kingdom on fire. Would he come out for that? Would he come out for me?" I asked as I looked in the mirror. "Are there any other formal complaints regarding his website right now?"

"No, there are none. Just yours. However, you have to understand his psychology. He is someone who would use someone else to attack you. He has been doing that for years - hiding behind a screen and playing his dirty games," Stephanie reasoned. "By the way, did you tell anyone about our plans?"

"Why would I? No, I didn't," I answered without hesitation.

"Are you sure? Think about it..."

I stopped, turned and opened the bathroom door. I looked Stephanie in the eye as I stood there with my towel wrapped around my moist body. "Well, maybe. I remember that I told another chatter that I was working on closing this app. That's all I said! I didn't give him any details of who, how, when and where," I explained in an uncomfortable manner.

"Damn! That's just enough reason for him to plan an exit. You shouldn't have mentioned this to anyone," she insisted. "Why would you..." she began to ask before realizing that I was in no state of mind to field such an obviously painful question.

I composed myself and gathered my thoughts. "I didn't reveal any pertinent information. I'm not a person who schemes and plots against other chatters or anyone in the real world either, for that matter. I'm straightforward and things are always black and white with me. Grey areas don't mix with my personality." I squinted and she nodded in agreement with what I said. "Well then, I don't know who you think you have in custody, but I do know this, if it's not Cobra, then I guarantee that he is not going to go anywhere - he is such an egotistical person. All logic will fail when it comes to his manly ego. He will be right here, hiding behind a different spy ID, recording each and every user. When it all settles down, he will begin attacking again.

Chapter Eleven

Bang Bang

I never thought that I would have to give up my life to remain alive. Everything that my father had toiled over from inception to perfection and everything that I had worked so hard to keep, was now out of my control and reach. I was reduced to being an observer through a phone app. It was so ironic in that it was a phone app that got me into this mess in the first place.

I sat on the cold leather of the unfamiliar couch in the apartment that I had tried to adjust to and become comfortable in. I just stared at my phone's screen, wishing that I was at my gallery and back with my friends in the city that I loved. I hated being relegated to living my life in hiding in the witness protection program; however, I shouldn't complain - my accommodations were nice, but they were not mine. Fortunately, I was in a financial position that didn't require me to immediately start a job. The FBI funneled some money out of my business account and transferred it to me anonymously so that I would have some stability. I was very lucky that the gallery was extremely solvent (especially after the auction event) and was able to survive and remain operational without me; however, it wasn't the cash that kept the gallery running. I desperately wanted to contact Dorothy and Mrs. Martha. If it hadn't been for the two of them stepping up in my absence and getting the gallery back up and running after the shooting, it would certainly still be closed today. They were both true friends indeed.

My days were long and lonely. I was frustrated and angry because I knew that every second that ticked by was a moment of my life that I could never relive or recoup. I tried to acquiesce to my new lifestyle and surroundings, but I just couldn't do it. On a couple of occasions, I went to a coffee shop or a restaurant by myself, but quickly left disappointed and uncomfortable. Oftentimes we take for granted all of the familiar things in our daily lives, never appreciating them until we are alienated.

I paced the room as I attempted to release my pent-up anxiety, unable to quell the anger within myself. I couldn't believe that I had been duped by Nick, Sam, Cobra - I felt like a gullible fool. And to think that I was falling in love with him. It would be a lie to say that I didn't need affection, because that is what I desperately needed right now - just from the right people.

~

Meanwhile, Dorothy pulled her car into the crowded parking lot of the police station and meandered her way through the assortment of both unmarked and marked police cars, finally finding a shady spot at the back of the lot. She took a deep breath as she looked in the rearview mirror and raised her brow in an attempt to lift the bags under her tired eyes. It was unlike her to ever leave the house without makeup on, but right now her barren face was the least of her concerns. A nervous feeling came over her, accompanied by slight nausea as she prepared herself for the worst. She sighed, even prayed for the first time in a long time as she exited the car and walked swiftly to the station. The air inside smelled like a cheap thrift store as the door swung open.

She surveyed the scene for a moment before walking over to the window surrounded by what she could only assume was bulletproof glass. She tapped the glass to get the attention of the burly and far-from-feminine woman officer. "I am here to see Detective Stephanie, um… I don't know her last name," she nervously inquired, hoping that there was only one detective named Stephanie working there.

The officer seemed bothered by her presence and reluctantly pointed from behind the glass and in the direction of a set of double doors across the lobby. Before Dorothy could ask anything else, the officer had already answered the phone that had been ringing. Dorothy wiped the sweat off of her forehead, turned and walked towards the doors where the officer had pointed. As the double doors swung open to reveal an institutionalized hallway and the glare of fluorescent light, she noticed a placard on one of the first office doors, indicating that she had found the right office. After a gentle knock on the open door, Stephanie raised her eyes from the mountain of paperwork on her desk to greet her visitor.

Dorothy forced a smile from her dry lips as she announced herself, "Hi Stephanie. I am Dorothy, Tanya's friend."

"Yes, Dorothy how can I help you?" she replied with an almost forced smile.

"Tanya has been missing for a couple of days. I didn't know where to go or what to do. I was hoping you could help me find her. I know she talks to you off and on. I thought maybe you might know something about where she is and what's going on. I'm so scared for her after the shooting at the gallery and all. This just isn't like her to disappear..."

Dorothy broke into tears as her emotions hit their melting point due to the sincere worry and concern for her missing friend. Stephanie pulled a tissue from her desk as she rose to console her desperate visitor with a brief hug.

"Yes, I am aware of the shooting incident. When did you last see her or talk to her?"

Dorothy composed herself and dried her tears. "We spoke the night of the shooting. She was with Nick. I spoke to them both briefly on the phone. The next day I went to her place to check on her, but she was not home and some of her clothes were missing. I went back multiple times later that day, but she never came home."

"Well," Stephanie said as she reached over and closed her office door for privacy, "Look, I know you are worried sick. So am I, but just know that she is safe. After the incident at her apartment, she was temporarily relocated for her own safety."

"Incident at her place?"

"Yes, there was an incident at her place. The FBI is involved now. It is out of my hands - I don't even know where she is now, but I do know that she is safe."

"I don't know much about this Nick guy that she was with. Can you please find out who he is?" Dorothy pleaded.

"They are working on that."

"They?"

"The FBI," Stephanie reassured her with a comforting rub on the back as Dorothy again began to cry.

"She doesn't have a family anymore. No one to look out for her. I'm her best friend and I want to be there for her, but I don't know where she is or what to do." Her soft cry turned into loud howl.

"Dorothy, it's going to be okay. I promise. The FBI is on it, but I'm going to have some of my guys look into this Nick Baker guy as well. He was at the auction that Tanya hosted. Can you please check at the gallery and see if you can find the buyer list and any other details that you can dig up on him for me? It would be a great help," Stephanie said, knowing full well that there was nothing there because the FBI had already swept the place after the shooting. She just thought that it may make Dorothy feel like she was helping and involved.

"Yes, I can get you that. I am sure his information will be on the buyer's list. I will come back tomorrow with all the information that I can find on him," Dorothy said with resolve as she began to turn toward the door.

"Hey," Stephanie said to halt her exit, "Would you like to watch Maggy?"

"She's here? Oh my God, yes!" The offer brought a smile to Dorothy's face as she quickly agreed. Stephanie buzzed someone on the phone and had them fetch the dog from the kennel. The reunion brought tears of joy to Dorothy's face and with the custody of her friend's furry friend, she left the station feeling slightly better than when she had arrived.

Dorothy headed straight to the gallery as Maggy hung her head out of the window to take in the fresh air, having just been liberated from incarceration at the police kennel. Upon arrival at the gallery, Dorothy burst into the back office and startled Mrs. Martha.

"Oh goodness, dear. You startled me," Mrs. Martha said as she suddenly broke her concentration from packing the remaining auction items that needed shipping.

"I'm sorry, I just wanted to stop by and see you."

"No worries, I've just been on pins and needles since the whole shooting and… Tanya."

"I know. That's why I wanted to stop by. I just spoke to her friend, the detective. She doesn't know where she is either, but she said that she is safe and implied that she is in a witness protection program and has been relocated by the FBI."

"Oh dear," Mrs. Martha sighed with concern on her face. "Oh hey, Maggy," she said as the dog came lagging into the office behind Dorothy.

"Yeah, they had her at the station. I'm going to dog-sit her until Tanya comes back home."

"Well, that's good," Mrs. Martha said with contained anxiety.

"What do we know about Nick?" Dorothy inquired as she took a seat across the desk from Mrs. Martha.

"I already checked everything we have, and it's not much. Gosh, I feel so terrible. I booked him for the auction - added him right in to the list. I feel deeply responsible. I didn't vet him properly. I mean, I ran a credit check, but…"

"Don't be hard on yourself, Mrs. Martha. It's not your fault. Deviants slip through no matter what," Dorothy said to ease her self-inflicted blame.

For hours, the two women combed their records as well as the internet, searching for information on Nick Baker. When they had both searched and exhausted every possible avenue, they simultaneously turned to the vault.

"Do you know the code?" Dorothy asked.

"Of course," she answered as she rose and walked across the office. Her fingers punched an alpha-numeric sequence into the keypad and then placed her index finger on the screen to satisfy the fingerprint recognition, an added level of security on the vault.

The lock released and Mrs. Martha pulled the door open. They both peered inside and saw the million-dollar painting that Nick had purchased sitting proudly and prominently in the safe. The sight sent chills down their spine and bewilderment through their minds.

~

"Bad cop, good cop routine?" the short FBI agent asked his tall counterpart as they walked down the hallway toward the interrogation room.

"How about bad cop, bad cop?" joked the taller agent. "Scum like this guy perpetrates child porn, identity theft and other online crimes. There's no good cop routine that's appropriate here."

"Right!" the shorter agent concurred as they swung the door open to the interrogation room.

The room was overly lit with fluorescent lighting which reflected obnoxiously off of the semi-gloss white walls. The only adornment on any of the walls was a glass panel, presumably a one-way window to allow for others to view the interrogation from behind a cloak of secrecy. In the middle of the room was a 3x6 metal table with 4 matching chairs - in which sat one handcuffed Nick Baker.

The shorter agent's voice echoed in the sterile room as he entered and said, "Let's get this party started," as he dropped a file loudly and forcefully on the end of the table opposite of Nick, who seemed unfazed by the two agents' dramatic entry.

"Let's start with your real name," the shorter agent said as he opened the file and pulled a pen from his jacket pocket, while the taller agent took his seat next to him.

"You tell me. You arrested me, booked me, fingerprinted me and detained me. You're the FBI, and you don't know who I am?" Nick said as arrogantly and defiantly as a handcuffed man could.

"Name," demanded the taller agent as he leaned across the table toward Nick.

"Attorney," Nick said as he locked eyes, his fist clenched as he glared in the direction of the tall agent.

"He thinks he's at the local lock-up on a drunk in public charge!" the tall agent laughed as he turned to the shorter agent. "There's no phone call here. Not until you answer some questions," he said with a stern demeanor as he turned his attention back to the prisoner.

"Fuck you," Nick said as he leaned across the table, matching the agent's demeanor with his tone and steely look.

"Look, we can play this game all day long, we're on the clock here," the short agent said as he closed the file and placed his pen on top of it. "You tell us who you are and answer our questions and then you'll get your phone call. Until we identify you, there's no phone call, Mr. Anonymous."

Nick remained silent and focused on the eyes of the tall agent across from him.

"Seriously man, we can sit here all day," the tall agent emphasized as he traded stares with the detainee.

After a few more moments of silence, Nick spoke in a slow, methodical and well enunciated tone, "I am a citizen. I have rights. I. Want. My. Attorney."

"You got nothing, pal," the tall agent chided. "You ever hear of the Patriot Act? Right now, you are a suspected cyber terrorist, buddy. You're not going anywhere or calling anyone until we ID you."

"Fuck you," Nick said as he rocked back in his chair in further defiance.

"Hey Fuck You, that's a great name," the shorter agent said as he grabbed his pen and pretended to write it on the file. "I'll refer to you as Fuck You from now on," he continued with a chuckle.

"I was thinking more along the lines of first name Ass, last name Hole," the tall agent interjected with a laugh.

"You know what, fuck this guy. He can rot," the short agent said as he slammed the pen down, grabbed the file and stood up.

"You can enjoy lockup until you decide to talk," the tall agent added as he stood up too and followed the short agent out of the room.

Nick remained seated and stoic until two other agents came in and escorted him back to his holding cell. He knew his record was clean. He doubted they currently had anything on him - and most importantly, he had committed no crime to warrant his arrest. But he would have plenty of time to contemplate his attitude in solitary confinement.

The two agents walked back to their office, slightly defeated, but confident that he would crack. When they returned to their desks, they found a note to call back detective Stephanie Oscar. The shorter agent took charge and picked up the black receiver of the standard-issued FBI desk phone. He dialed the handwritten number on the memo.

"Hi, this is agent Schmidt from the FBI, returning your call."

"Thanks for responding so quickly," the detective replied. "What have you got on him?"

"Nothing so far. He's not talking. His fingerprints came back clean - he's not in our system. He had no identification on his person or in his vehicle, which was rented under the name of Nick Baker who resides at a fake address and pays in cash. He's in custody until we identify him. He's definitely got something to hide."

"Huh," Stephanie sighed. "I'm just wondering how long Tanya will have to remain in relocation. Her friend stopped by today to file a missing person report. I handled that for now though, but we can't keep Tanya away from her life for long, plus she's well-known around town - if she's gone long, people will start wondering why."

~

These were certainly the longest days of my life. I went through the motions each day, barely eating and definitely not engaging in any kind of worthwhile activities. Short of catching up on some soap operas and a few sitcoms, my time had been utterly unproductive - a dismal experience for a go-getter and an entrepreneur like myself. Not a moment went by when I didn't question, at the back of my mind, my decision to blow the whistle on Sam and his website. My real pain originated from the decision to log on to iVoice in the first place. I tried not to beat myself up about it.

How could the FBI take a Florida girl from Tampa and move her to the mountains of North Carolina? It is still cold here. Beautiful, but cold. I despise the cold. There is nothing to do. No desire to meet anyone. No aspiration to continue with the drama and this interruption of normal life.

Against all protocol, I picked up the FBI issued smart phone and dialed Stephanie's number from memory.

"I want to come home," I pleaded when she answered on the third ring.

There was no need for introduction or formality, Stephanie knew who it was right away. She also knew that I must be ready to cave in and return home in order for me to make such a bold move as to call her against strict orders from the FBI.

"I know you do, Tanya. Listen, the FBI is working on it. I've also got a few detectives in my office working on it for me as well. But right now, we have nothing on the man in custody, this so-called Nick Baker. He is coming up clean and he isn't talking. You really need to lay low and be patient right now until we figure out who he is and what his connection is to the men who shot at you. You are jeopardizing your safety right now. Let's keep this brief. I promise you I will do my best on this case to expedite your return to safety here."

And with that, Tanya pushed the button on the phone to end the call.

~

The detective flashed her credentials at the security gate and was allowed entry into the government complex after a brief inquisition from the security guard. She made her way through the labyrinth of a parking lot, passing an assortment of cars ranging from government tagged vehicles that were clearly FBI issued, to exotic sports cars, possibly confiscated from criminals. She found an open spot up front, parked and sauntered into the secure vestibule of the sophisticated building, which was a far cry from her antiquated police department. In fact, even the crisp sterility of the air inside made her question her decision to make the career choice of a local detective versus an FBI agent. The security guard verified her credentials and notified agent Schmidt that she had arrived. She was escorted into the building and to a private and well-appointed meeting room. Within minutes, both agent Schmidt and his taller counterpart entered the room.

"Detective, thanks for stopping by," the shorter agent said as he extended his arm and greeted her with a firm handshake.

"My pleasure. Tanya is restless and is ready to return. I need to know that she is safe if she does in fact return."

The tall agent spoke up, "Detective, we've interrogated the suspect numerous times over the last few weeks. We've gotten nowhere. He is maintaining silence other than demanding an attorney. He's not well. Not eating."

"We just can't figure out why he's holding out. It's certainly an admission of guilt. But we are treading on thin ice holding him any longer with no evidence and no formal charges. We've bluffed him as best as we can, but to no avail," the vertically challenged agent disclosed.

The detective drummed her fingers on the desk and focused her eyes in deep contemplation as if she was looking through both the agents with x-ray vision. "I would like a minute alone with the prisoner."

The taller agent immediately objected, probably feeling threatened by the notion of a mere detective, a woman no less, doing his job on his turf. But the shorter agent relented, conceding that there was no harm in trying a different angle.

The three of them stood peering through the one-way glass of the interrogation room as the gaunt and emaciated prisoner was escorted into the room in handcuffs, his orange jumpsuit hanging on his frame with plenty of fabric to spare. His appearance was quite a contrast to the last time the detective had seen him weeks prior.

"Kill the cameras and turn off the mic," the detective said as she entered the room solo. The taller agent again objected, but the shorter officer obliged.

The agents peered through the glass as Stephanie sat down quietly and calmly across from the sullen detainee. The agents attempted to read the lips of both of them during the private interrogation, but for the most part, they were unsuccessful. What they did observe was a dramatic shift in the attitude and demeanor of the prisoner. Within 15 minutes, the detective emerged from the room, smiled and proceeded to brief the agents on her findings.

"His name is Aaron Thompson," she said as they returned to the posh meeting room. "He lives at 111 Walden Street #945 in New York," she relayed as she read her own notes aloud. "The combination to his front door lock is 5647. In the top right dresser drawer in the master bedroom, you will find his US passport and birth certificate."

"Fucking unbelievable," the taller agent mumbled in disbelief. "How did you…"

"That's not all," the detective said as she interrupted the agent. "Here are the physical addresses and IP addresses for Monica Girard and Sam Baker. He is willing to testify against them and their involvement in the porn site in exchange for his release and amnesty. As for the two men who shot at him and Tanya in front of the gallery, he swears he is not involved with them, nor has he ever seen them before. I'm inclined to believe him."

"Seriously, how did you pull that off?" the shorter agent asked in amazement.

"Woman's touch," she said as she smiled and dismissed herself from their presence.

~

My FBI issued smart phone rang and the caller ID came up 'unavailable'. I hesitated, but answered the phone anyway.

"Hi, Tanya. It's agent Schmidt."

"Yes, agent Schmidt. It's good to finally hear from you. What news do you have for me?"

"Well, I understand that you are eager to return home and resume your normal life."

"Yes, that's true," I said with excitement as my spirit rose.

"There has been some progress and new developments in our investigation. We are in the process of positively identifying Nick Baker. We have credible evidence that we are processing right now. Although we have not apprehended the two men involved in the shooting, we feel that we are getting close. We would advise you to stay put longer until we piece everything together."

"How long are we talking? Days? Weeks?"

"Unfortunately, I cannot answer that question honestly or accurately right now. It could be tomorrow or it could be months from now."

"Oh," I said with disappointment. "I can't go on like this much longer. I'm not enjoying this sedentary lifestyle and I'm becoming consumed with anger. I want my life back!"

"I understand. Remember, you are in a *voluntary* program. You can leave at any time. My priority is your safety and I must advise you accordingly."

"Thank you for your honesty - I appreciate that. But I want to come home now."

"Okay then, pack up your personal items. I will arrange for a transport to pick you up Thursday at noon and drive you back to Tampa. I want to be clear though, if you come back now, you're still at risk and you're taking your life into your own hands."

"Understood," I said as I hung up the phone with a smile. I resolved to have faith in the fact that I could defend myself.

~

The transport delivered me to the FBI headquarters in Tampa for re-entry processing, where I was delighted to discover that Stephanie was there to greet me.

"Welcome back home!" Stephanie said as she embraced me with a huge hug. It was the first human contact that I had experienced in almost a month. "You did great, now come…" she said as she directed me to the meeting room for debriefing.

I walked in slowly to find the two familiar FBI officers waiting for me. They both greeted me with pretentious smiles. They then proceeded to show me evidence such as a passport, lie detector test, voice recognition and more that substantiated that Nick Baker was, in fact, Aaron Thompson. The tall agent rambled on and on, recounting the methods they had used to procure the information; all the while Stephanie sat quietly and listened, letting them take all the credit.

"He claims he was just trying to protect you and he denies association with the two men who attempted to shoot the two of you. He is also willing to testify against the real Sam Baker and his accomplices," agent Schmidt interjected.

I objected, "Are you guys crazy?" I went on to explain how so many things pointed to the fact that he was

Sam/Cobra. I cited that fact that he called me Wildcat as my most credible evidence. “Sam was the *only* person who called me Wildcat,” I reasoned.

The taller agent cut me off and said, “Well, as credible as it may seem to you, we cannot detain or convict someone based on the fact that they happened to call you by a certain name.”

I was not happy and I let them know it. “I want to see the interrogation feed. It's my right. If you don't show it to me, I will have my attorney call you.”

I continuously insisted that I wanted to see the feed right away and that I wasn’t going home until I did. The agents explained to me that Aaron was in a federal detention facility and all of the proceedings and questioning were done there, thus making it classified information. They also informed me that a psych evaluation was done and he was cleared for release. In the next few days he would be processed and released, pending the examination of all evidence and testimonials.

I was irate, but Stephanie calmed me down as she escorted me out of the FBI complex and then gave me and all of my stuff a ride home. On the ride home, Stephanie surprisingly sided with the FBI’s findings and assured me that the man in custody was definitely not who I thought he was. I didn’t have it in me to argue with her any further, so I didn’t. I was just thrilled to be back home and to be with her at the moment. She helped me unload all of my stuff and carry it into my house. She offered to stay with me, but I thanked her for her help and declined her offer.

The first thing I did was to plug *my* phone into the charger and power it up for the first time in a month. It was too late to call Mrs. Martha, so I planned to see her at the gallery the following morning. I immediately dialed up Dorothy though.

She answered on the second ring and the excitement in her voice almost blew my left ear drum out. "Oh my God! It's you! Where have you been?"

"I am fine. I am back now. I missed you so much."

"I want to see you. I will come over RIGHT NOW!" she exclaimed, clearly overwhelmed with the fact that I was back in town.

"Sure. Come on over. I would love to have your company."

While I impatiently waited for her to arrive, I busied myself with dusting off furniture and even vacuumed the carpet. I opened the refrigerator and stared at the empty shelves. I guess it's pizza tonight, I thought as I dialed up the local delivery parlor. As I continued to tidy up, I noticed that the FBI bugs were still present throughout my house. I texted Stephanie to see when they would be removed.

Suddenly, I heard the doorbell ring and I rushed towards the door, assuming it to be Dorothy. As I placed my hand on the door knob, I thought to myself what if it was

Sam? Regardless, I swung the door open anyway to discover the extremely speedy pizza delivery guy. I was certain that the next knock on the door would be Dorothy - and it was!

"Oh! Sweetheart!" Dorothy cried as she embraced me. Maggy came rushing in behind her, barking with joy.

"I am good. Nothing happened to me," I said as Dorothy held me in a bear hug in the doorway. "Come in, I have pizza - and a lot to tell you!"

I proceeded to regale her with all the details of the happenings (and lack thereof) that had happened over the last month as she sat there listening in disbelief, while Maggy tried to lick my face off. Dorothy was a bit scared and intimidated by the fact that the house was still bugged. She couldn't believe that someone had actually tried to kill me in front of the gallery.

"So, who exactly shot you?" she asked in a confused tone as she took another bite of the pizza.

"I believe that Nick Baker, or should I say, Sam or Cobra, was connected somehow to the men who tried to shoot me."

"That's impossible! How could you know for sure?"

"I just know it. I can feel it in my bones. He called me Wildcat. I haven't shared that with anyone. Sam/Cobra was the only one who knew that."

"Well, he could have shared that with Aaron or Monica or anyone else for that matter!" she said in Nick's defense.

"Doubtful. He said it was 'our little secret'."

"Do you still believe anything that Sam said? He conned you repeatedly."

"I don't know what to believe, but I do believe my gut instinct and it tells me that I'm right. Plus, there was the limo incident."

"Limo incident?"

"Yes, on the ride home after the night at the club when the three of us were celebrating the auction event. I was drunk out of my mind and I was in and out of consciousness. I'm certain that we left the club in his car, but I woke up momentarily in the back of a limo with Nick and two men who looked just like the two guys who tried to shoot us. My memory is foggy, but I've had a lot of time to think about it and piece together all of the details."

"Really? Oh my God," Dorothy said in shock.

I held my head in both hands and closed my eyes in dismay. I wasn't sure what to do next. I certainly didn't feel like carrying on this conversation or battle any longer. I was unclear what I was fighting for at this time - closing down the porn site, shutting down the app, putting Aaron and Sam in jail.

“But why did you take things into your own hands? It wasn't required,” Dorothy delicately inquired.

I sat in quiet thought for a moment, reflecting on how to answer the question. “Dorothy, I can't be a mere spectator of wrongdoings. Should I react when something bad happens to me? And is it acceptable to stand by idly if something bad is happening to someone else? I have read about school shootings, young adults committing suicide or suffering from depression, dropping out of school or college for drugs and gangs. Should I be blind to all of it, if it is not happening to me? If each one of us can do our part in the right way, we may not have as many of these situations in the world today. It's impossible to get rid of all the negativity and wrongdoings, but a little positive effort from each of us can create a huge difference in the world and maybe save young lives. Never in my life have I succumbed to a bully or let one have their way with innocent people around me. These creeps with their games and online antics needed to be stopped. I stepped up and did the right thing.”

She sat in silence and listened to my every word as I continued, “Dorothy, should I have waited until these men did something wrong to you? After which, I would feel obligated to react anyway. It’s my responsibility as a friend or just a concerned citizen. I would look out for a complete stranger as well.”

“I know you would. And that is what makes you a dear friend and a very special person.” She didn't have anything else to say at the moment. She just rubbed me on my shoulder and hugged me some more.

"Don't worry anymore. Get some sleep. I am proud of you and what you did. It takes a lot of courage to selflessly pursue a remedy to wrongdoings - especially in the face of such danger. I am glad to have you back and I'm glad you are my friend. You need to rest your mind now. I will meet you at the gallery tomorrow to go over everything that happened there since you've been gone."

"Please stay. I don't want to be alone."

"Sure thing. I would love that."

After I took a shower and we ate the rest of the pizza, we settled down to watch some TV. I flipped through the channels and found the most comical and nonsensical thing I could find, a Tom and Jerry cartoon - perfect for my mood. I fell asleep on the couch after giggling through part of the show. Dorothy grabbed a pillow and a throw blanket for me and made sure I was comfortable. She stayed right next to me all cuddled up until morning.

We woke up, dressed up and she drove me to the gallery. It felt so good to walk into my father's old office again - and this time, I got to surprise Mrs. Martha. She cried tears of joy when she saw me after so long. It was an emotional reunion and she spent the next few hours catching me up on all the happenings at the gallery, praising Dorothy over and over again for her help in my absence.

After a long, emotional day at the gallery, I asked Dorothy and Mrs. Martha to go home and take a break. All of this was taking a toll on the three of us. They were both reluctant to leave me, but I assured them I would be okay. I pried open my purse far enough for them to see the FBI issued gun that I still had in my possession.

I was the last one to leave the building and I called for a taxi. On the ride home, I thought about all of the calls and emails that I had to catch up on the next day. It would take days before I could possibly feel caught up. I got home, paid the taxi driver, emptied the mailbox and strolled into my house. I was greeted by a very happy Maggy who desperately needed to go outside for a potty break.

As we strolled around the block, this feeling of being watched ran through my mind and sent chills up my spine. I dismissed the thought as paranoia, but encouraged Maggy to expedite her business and then we promptly returned home. I fumbled through my bag as my keys were nowhere to be found. I dropped a few things from my bag onto the front porch. I bent down to pick them up after releasing Maggy's leash from her collar. I discovered my keys at the bottom of the purse and as I rose with them in my hand to unlock the door, I noticed that Maggy had already pushed her way through the front door and run into the house. Huh, I was certain that I had locked the door. I walked inside, carefully locking the door behind me. I walked over to the kitchen and grabbed a glass to fill with water from the fridge. Suddenly, I heard a loud thump sound followed by Maggy's barking in the other room. I turned just in time to see a shadow moving on the far side of the room. I instinctively reached for my purse that I had just laid on the kitchen counter, snatching it up and dumping its contents out. The gun landed prominently on the granite with a thud, but it didn't stay there long as I grabbed it, cocked it and pointed it in the direction of the shadow. For a hot second, I wondered if it could possibly be Dorothy, Stephanie or one of the FBI agents, but then a familiar face came into the light.

"How dare you come here?" I said as I clutched the gun firmly, bringing the intruder into my sight.

"Calm down, I am here to talk. Put the gun down, please."

"Are you *really* here to talk? I think you are here to kill me."

"No, I'm not. Trust me. It was Sam."

I tried to conceal my trembling arm by gripping the gun tighter and elongating my reach toward him. "Stop lying - you are Sam. You can't fool me. I know both of you well."

He started to approach me from around the couch, but I held the gun high and firm and demanded that he stopped. He understood my seriousness and stopped dead in his tracks. He tried to explain how he had met Monica at a party and how she had tricked him into moving in with him, only later to cheat on him with Sam who had been blackmailing her with the porn website. He said that when he confronted Sam about me, he shot him.

"You're a liar. I don't believe you. You said Wild Cat."

"Well, I know that from Sam, he shared a file on you with me. He sent me information on you."

"I *knew* that you were involved with him. Shame on you! You have no remorse." My nostrils flared with anger and my heart pounded.

"Tanya, I wanted to protect you from Sam. At the same time, I couldn't reveal myself because you wouldn't believe my true intentions. After Sam shot me, he teamed up with Monica again and tipped the cops off about me. I was on the run. Sam told me he is onto you and I couldn't let it happen to you, what he did to me."

"I don't believe you. I don't believe any of what you are saying. Why did you call me Wild Cat? Did you know the FBI had my house bugged? Did you sweep my house?" I could feel myself hyperventilating as I tried to catch my breath. My heart was spinning and I felt as if I would burst into tears at any moment, but I didn't - I held strong and firm.

"Please believe me. I truly…." he said as he briefly looked away.

"I truly...what?" I asked, moving a step closer to him as he turned his back to me. I needed to look into his eyes, and demanded, "Turn towards me, look me in the eye and say it."

"I love you. What I did was out of love for you!" he pleaded as he turned back, reached his hand out and moved a step closer to me.

I stepped back and choked back my tears, "You need to answer me. Did you know what I was doing?" I demanded as I brandished the gun.

"Yes, I did. It didn't matter to me. He knows it as well!" he said, looking away in dismay again.

"I don't believe any of it. I want you to leave right now."

"I am saying I love you. Don't you understand that? And you're making me leave?" he said as he moved closer towards me.

"Don't get near me. Stay away. I'm gonna shoot you!" I affirmed as I tensed my hands, preparing to pull the trigger. I squinted my left eye as I looked down the sight over the barrel of the gun. "I know you are Sam and I know you killed Aaron and took his identity. We did a background check on you for the auction."

"Tanya, put the gun down. I can show you I am Aaron and not Sam," he said as he reached into his pocket and took a step closer.

"No, don't. I am gonna shoot, I don't know if you have a gun," I screamed as I glanced down for a split second to see what appeared to be a bulge in his pants' pocket. "STOP!"

"It's just a piece of paper. Let me show you."

His elbow began to bend as he started to slowly withdraw his hand from his pocket.

"STOP. I WILL SHOOT."

Time stood still for me. It was the longest split second of my life.

BANG. BANG.

ACKNOWLEDGEMENT

I would like to thank God for my beautiful mind and near perfect body.

I would like to thank my family, friends, schoolmates, college mates and everyone else who lent an ear and provided feedback on this creation. I would also like to thank the online community and a handful of chat buddies who have been supportive throughout. With much appreciation and gratitude, I would like to thank my editor Sean Donovan and my advisor and publisher, Kevin Snyder for their help in bringing this story to life.